HEADSHOT

ALSO BY RITA BULLWINKEL

Belly Up: Stories

HEADSHOT

RITA BULLWINKEL

PICADOR INDIA

First published 2024 by Daunt Books,
United Kingdom
First published in India 2024 by Picador India
an imprint of Pan Macmillan Publishing India Private Limited
707 Kailash Building
26 K. G. Marg, New Delhi 110001
www.panmacmillan.co.in

Pan Macmillan, The Smithson, 6 Briset Street, Farringdon, London EC1M 5NR
Associated companies throughout the world
www.panmacmillan.com

ISBN 978-93-6113-624-5

This is a work of fiction. Names, characters, businesses, organizations, places, events, and incidents either are the product of the author's imagination or are used fictitiously. Any resemblance to actual persons, living or dead, events, or locales is entirely coincidental.

1 3 5 7 9 8 6 4 2

Typeset in Quadraat by Marsha Swan
Printed and bound in India by Thomson Press India Ltd.

MIX
Paper | Supporting responsible forestry
FSC® C010615
FSC www.fsc.org

For my sister, Audrey, witness to it all

From ‘Games for Girls’ by ancient history scholar Thomas F. Scanlon

Only after the classical period did Greek girls come to compete in men’s athletic festivals. References to this are few and late, suggesting exceptional social circumstances . . . A first-century AD inscription found at Delphi records young women who personally competed in chariot races or footraces . . . Yet these girls probably competed only against other girls, as in a race for daughters . . .

The 12th Annual

WOMEN'S 18 & UNDER

DAUGHTERS OF AMERICA CUP

—at—

BOB'S BOXING PALACE

—in—

RENO, NV

JULY 14TH–JULY 15TH 20XX

JULY 14

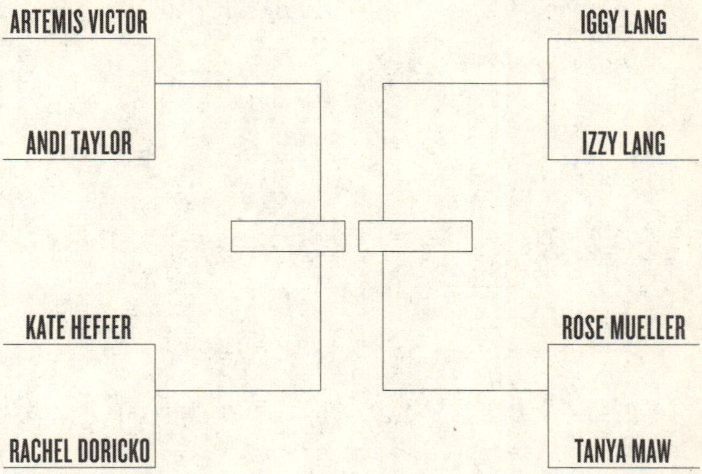
ARTEMIS VICTOR
ANDI TAYLOR
KATE HEFFER
RACHEL DORICKO
IGGY LANG
IZZY LANG
ROSE MUELLER
TANYA MAW

ARTEMIS VICTOR
VS.
ANDI TAYLOR

Andi Taylor is pumping her hands together, hitting her own flat stomach, thinking not of her mother sitting at home with her little brother, not of her car, which barely got her here, not of her summer job, her lifeguarding at the overcrowded community pool, not of the four-year-old she watched die, the four-year-old she practically killed, and his blue cheeks. They shouldn't give teenagers the job of saving children. It doesn't matter how many CPR classes you've taken. She killed the boy with her wandering eyes. His swimsuit had small red trucks on it. He looked like he was made out of plastic. The feel of his thigh when she pulled him from the bottom of the pool, already dead, and the way it was so easy to grip, because it was so small, she's not thinking about it. She's looking at the skylight and the light it's letting in on this shit-hole gym and she's thinking about the things she always does wrong when she fights, her lazy left guard, the way her left hand slips away and doesn't protect her face if she's not thinking about it. She is also thinking about the way Artemis Victor will get her. If Andi Taylor doesn't think about this, this fight will be over in a matter of seconds. Andi Taylor needs to think about her spacing and her stomach. Andi Taylor needs to think about her stance.

They're still sitting and looking at each other meanly. They know each other but have never fought before. When you join the women's youth boxing league this facade of a sports association makes you pay two hundred dollars and then you get a 'free' subscription to their magazine, which profiles its members, young girl boxers, one by one, so you see who's out there, even if they are across the country, and you get a good sense of who you're up against, and you know who they've fought and who they are going to fight and what their favourite hobby is because god only knows what kind of a journalist writes this excuse for a magazine, but whoever it is seems to think it is valuable information and that it should be included in every athlete profile, because in every issue there it is: name, hometown, favourite colour, hobby, wins and losses, photo of the girl in gloves. The photo is a wild card because some girls choose to take it in their gym clothes, while others choose to take it in halter tops, their hair down, their heads tilted, and their gloves resting on their hips.

Andi Taylor would know Artemis Victor anywhere because Artemis Victor is the youngest of the three Victor sisters, a family of boxers whose parents come to every single one of Artemis's matches with shirts that say 'Victor', which is, of course, ridiculous, their proclamation of their daughters' winning records on their chests.

Everyone knows the Victor sisters and what they've won and what they've lost and the judges treat Artemis's family like old friends, which, in boxing, is especially infuriating because the grey area of a call is often so present, and if you know a judge has a special relationship with the participants, you can't help thinking, I'm being slighted, this is the end of me, if only I had parents willing to befriend my coaches, if only I had parents who could get off work, who didn't work, who could come see me win.

•

Mr and Mrs Victor sit in folding chairs next to the ring. There are barely over two dozen other onlookers: judges, other girl fighters, a journalist from the local paper, a journalist from the Women's Youth Boxing Association magazine, parents, a grandmother, coaches, and Bob, the owner of this gym.

•

Bob is also a coach, but, as a rule, doesn't coach women. He has no particular fighter he'd like to see win. His gym was just the right location for the tournament to take place. All the coaches are men and all the coaches own gyms, and all the coaches collect fees from the girls to, in part, pay the Women's Youth Boxing Association, who, in turn, pays the coaches for hosting regionals at their gyms. Some of the coaches were amateur boxers, but many of them have never competed at the level that these girls are fighting in. The girls' coaches travel to the tournament to get their cheques from the association. In between rounds, Artemis's and Andi's coaches do speak to them, but the coaches speak only in clichés and useless information. Everything the coaches have taught the girls is in the past. The language of the coaches inside Bob's Boxing Palace is like the sound of the loud overhead fan. Artemis and Andi wish they could fight with less sound pollution. Every sound other than the smack of a hit is only a distraction.

•

Artemis Victor is rolling her shoulders. She's looking at Andi Taylor and thinking, You are ugly. I am prettier than you and I am going to beat you, too.

Artemis sizes up other women physically everywhere. I'm the prettiest woman in this room, she thinks. There's one woman, over there, who may be prettier, if you like girls who look like drug addicts. There are men who like girls who look like drug addicts. When Artemis Victor thinks of herself in the future, she thinks of herself as wildly successful in a big house, maybe in Miami, not a drug addict. Artemis Victor has a teddy bear that has a doll's shirt that says 'Victor'.

'That's my girl!' yells Mrs Victor.

•

Artemis Victor always thinks she is going to win. It's not a bad habit to get in. If one is capable of throwing self-doubt out the window, this power can be a beneficial weapon to deploy. Artemis Victor hates her oldest sister. Her oldest sister won the Daughters of America Cup four years ago. Her middle sister got a silver. Even if Artemis wins the whole thing, wins the whole tournament and becomes the best in the country, the best woman under eighteen in the United States at boxing, she'll still be second best to her oldest sister, Star Victor, because Star became the best in the country before her and is now married with a husband and a child and well on her way to owning a house if not being rich.

•

Artemis Victor has no idea what it takes to own a house, but she knows what it takes to beat other people, which is what owning property seems like, beating other people at owning a piece of the earth and making that piece of earth yours, not to be shared with other people, because the owning of the property is a product of your victory over other humans, as in, you won more dollars than them so now this slice of land is yours for keeps.

•

It's not that Artemis Victor is stupid. She'd make an excellent banker, though she'll become a wine distributor. It's just that her values are very narrow. She has an insanely good eye for reading people, for knowing what they are thinking under the words they are speaking, for watching how people hold themselves when they talk to you, whether or not they are interested in you. She knows which of her high school teachers to feel bad for: the ones whose eyes dart around looking for someone to listen to them. She knows the right way to say a thing to make people think she is interested in hearing them speak.

Artemis Victor is also a vegan. She genuinely feels bad for animals. This was part of her profile in the Women's Youth Boxing Association magazine (the *WYBA*). Artemis Victor loves animals. She watched a documentary on the abuse of whales in theme parks and also thinks they should be set free.

•

The referee is in the middle of the ring and is saying things to the girls about rules that they already know and have heard a hundred times before. They nod their heads and get up off their stools and begin to bounce up and down. Andi is bouncing much more than Artemis. Artemis paces forward, steady. They're both wearing silk shorts and sports bras and tank tops. The elastic on their waistbands makes dents in their skin that will last for hours after they take their shorts off.

A week ago, Andi came home and took off her shorts and looked at the red ring of gullies the shorts had left on her stomach. She fingered the indentations with her hands. When the marks disappeared an hour later she was sad to not have them. They seemed like evidence of the work she'd done. She wished she had a black eye from a winning fight to wear around, to show people she was fighting, to show people her body was doing something that was hard.

•

Andi's knee is out too far and Artemis moves in to force Andi to retract it back under her hips. These are the size-up seconds – the moments a fighter has to see if and where their opponent has weaknesses.

If Artemis has a weakness it is in the fact that she is a legacy. Her sisters' wins hang over her. She is reminded of them constantly. This is the tournament where she can be as good as her eldest sister, or the worst boxer in their family. The type of legacy that is the Victor family is rarer in boxing than in other kinds of sports, but not unheard of. Youth women's boxing is a world small enough that the Victors could conquer it.

•

Andi Taylor's knee is still not in the right place. Artemis lifts her lip up to her nose to show her red mouth guard-covered teeth.

•

Artemis's biceps are balls of muscle. She can hit things harder than most people can throw a ball. Her back muscles are arched in two small hills on either side of her neck. Artemis begins to see a weakness in the way Andi moves where Artemis thinks she can place a hit. Artemis Victor thinks she can touch Andi Taylor. Just as Artemis thinks this, Andi hits the left side of Artemis Victor's ribs.

It's a hard blow that the judges call a hit immediately. The score is yelled loud enough so everyone can hear it. This is a point-hitting game, after all. That's why they wear padded headgear that circles their ears and cheeks and foreheads and buckles under their chins. This is target practice.

Andi had seen a tunnel of a vacancy between her right fist and Artemis's left rib cage. It had looked illuminated, like it was just begging to be filled with Andi's fist. Andi had put her hand in the hole to Artemis's body, that tunnel of vacancy, and then was filling the hole again, and again, until the referee got between them.

•

The referee had checked the inside of Andi's gloves before he taped them onto her wrists. He was checking to see if she had put lead in them. They always do this before a match. It's part of the rules of the association.

•

Andi loves when the referees reach into her gloves. She likes watching their hands go into a hole where her hands are about to go. The fact that they check every time makes Andi feel like she is capable of murder. She loves having an adult confirm that her fist could be a weapon. Maybe she could put a rock in there. Maybe she is capable of killing the girl she is fighting. Every time the referees look in her gloves it is like they are saying, You are capable of killing, which feels good to Andi. Most people in her life don't seem to believe she is capable of anything, let alone killing someone with purpose, and with the wandering-eyes murder of the little boy, she wonders if she is also capable of killing someone with her fists.

•

The boy with the red-truck shorts Andi wasn't thinking about him, was not even the worst thing that had happened to Andi, or the first dead body she had seen. But, it was the smallest (the other dead body had been her father's). The smallness of the dead boy had seemed especially disgusting. The day had been so clear and dry. She hadn't cried. She vomited after it was clear that the red-truck kid was not going to come back to life. The vomiting made Andi feel like she herself was a small child. She was surprised by her body's visceral repulsion to the dead red-truck kid. It was the image of his small, corn-dog-sized thigh that made her vomit. Andi hit Artemis again, this time on Artemis's shoulder. How long could she get away with hitting Artemis Victor?

•

Bob's Boxing Palace had been selected for the Daughters of America Cup because of its central location, the fact that it was vaguely in the middle of the American heartland, or was, at least, not near an ocean, and because Bob was the brother of the head of the Women's Youth Boxing Association, which collected one hundred dollars from each entrant to pay the referees, the judges, and the facility fees, and the association officials for their time.

•

Andi had used her lifeguarding money to pay the entry fee, which now seemed like blood money.

•

There was always a qualifying, regional Daughters of America Cup before the national one, so the WYBA collected fees from over one thousand young women, which means that they did make a profit, usually fifty or sixty thousand dollars, and Bob got to take some of that home for having it at his run-down gym.

•

The difference between Artemis Victor's and Andi Taylor's bodies was that Artemis was thicker. The muscles stuck out from her arms and her back like there were ropes under her skin. In Artemis's forearms there were clear lines of sinew from her wrists to her elbows. Her shoulders were broad, and looked especially large when she crammed them into strapless dresses. During fights she always wore makeup. Artemis wore waterproof mascara and a red stain on her lips.

•

Andi was tall and gangly. She had a cross-country runner's body. People were always telling her she should try running long distances. She wasn't interested.

•

Artemis Victor had the archetype of a ponytail. She had so much brown hair it barely fit in one rubber band. When she wasn't fighting she wore it either on the side or in a big bun on top of her head. Even up, it was still long enough to brush against her shoulders. She always said she was growing it out to cut off and give to a girl with cancer, but she never cut her hair except in small, two- or three-inch trims.

•

The stylists at the salon Artemis goes to never seem to listen. Don't cut too much, she tells them. I need it long, she says to them. She always leaves the salon feeling like some part of herself has been stolen.

•

Andi Taylor's hair was so thin that when she braided the whole of it, the braid was as small as her index finger. When her hair got wet it felt slimy. Andi Taylor worried about her hair breaking off when it was really cold out. It had happened once, just with a couple of strands, but she had so little hair that it felt very dramatic, like she had lost something in short supply that she would never get back.

•

The fact of the two girls' bodies was not lost on Artemis Victor or Andi Taylor or on any of the young women in the Daughters of America tournament. Their bodies were the only tools they had at their disposal. This wasn't lacrosse or tennis. There were no rackets. They had their arms and their legs and their headgear-clad heads and their glove-covered hands, although the gloves and the headgear were just there as protective measures, to make sure they didn't kill each other. The gloves and the head-gear weren't something they needed to perform the skill they had practised, though they did, in their separate states, in their separate gyms, all practise with gloves and headgear. The gloves and the headgear were like clothing. One could box with them, or without them, just as one could, technically, swim naked or in a suit.

•

Andi Taylor and Artemis Victor looked at each other's bodies under the roof of Bob's Boxing Palace and tried to figure out how they could make their fists touch each other's faces. This was the first match of the tournament, the semi-finalist round. If you lost, you were out. There was no back door in the Daughters of America.

•

Andi advanced towards Artemis with her right foot out in front, dragging her left leg behind her. It was an inelegant, inefficient strut that got her where she needed to go, just not very prettily. Andi had never been concerned with the brokenness of her form. She didn't know about the many problems that could come with advancing so off-balance. Andi opened so much of her right side up to her opponent this way. She was walking like a crab. It was a stupid way to box. It was weird. As in, it looked weird to Artemis. None of Artemis's sisters boxed like this. Andi was tremendously off-balance, so

Artemis swung at her. Artemis's glove touched Andi's chest. The referee called the hit.

•

The way Andi's body recovered from the blow was even stranger than her off-kilter advance forward. She had leaned into it, which seemed somewhat impossible. But Andi had, in fact, seen the hit coming, and, though too late to move her whole body, she had been able to move back, slightly, out of the way of the full impact of Artemis's fist.

•

Andi saw Artemis's glove hit her chest more than she felt it. She saw the red fabric of the glove move under her eyes and in between her shoulders. It was like she was flying over a red piece of fabric. Andi was on top of the red ocean. She pulled away and started her advance towards Artemis again.

•

The difference between them as fighters was greater than the difference between them as people. Artemis's form was polished and calculated. Andi hit carelessly. Her hands moved slowly, but in strange directions.

•

There is a glorification, in the world outside of boxing, of desperation and wildness while fighting – this notion that desire and scrappiness can and will conquer experience. No boxing coach has ever asked their athlete to be more desperate. Control and restraint are much more valuable than wild punches.

•

Andi wasn't sure why the sight of her father's dead body had upset her so much less than the sight of the dead red-truck kid. It could have been because the boy's body was evidence of an unlived life. Perhaps it was also because Andi felt she had killed the boy. Had Andi killed the boy? Both bodies had been obvious surprises. Her father had died on the couch watching television. He had lived in an apartment, divorced from Andi's mother, and lived alone. When Andi found her father it was just her and the dead version of him, her alone with the corpse upon entry. She thought of them there together, her entering the apartment and her father having missed the last hour, his favourite hour, of television, already dead before the episode had even had a chance to begin.

•

The fact that Andi had felt two corpses (Artemis had felt zero) mattered zero while they were trying to hit each other's bodies. They were both young girls who grew up being treated as young women, which unified their lived experiences more greatly than any family (or witnessed) tragedy. It was not as if women's boxing was, or ever had, or ever would be something respected enough to put every ounce of your energy into. The practice took its toll on both Artemis's and Andi's bodies. The sweat that hung in between Andi's forehead and her headgear gave her acne that she had to cover up with foundation. She looked terrible in bangs, but she cut her hair with bangs anyway, to hide the way the headgear plastic made her break out into deep, subterranean zits. She'd got a staph infection in one of the zits once, from touching her face after touching some of the lifting equipment at the gym where she practised. The bacteria had rotted a pea-sized hole into her forehead for a full week before her mother insisted she go to the doctor. The doctor had to shoot Andi up with extra-strength penicillin and then the staph infection had scabbed over, leaving what looked like a dead bug on her forehead for nearly six weeks.

And not to mention the broken bones they both have, mostly in their fingers. Both Artemis and Andi have broken their fists loads of times, but Artemis's fists have been broken a dozen more times than Andi's, and, though Artemis doesn't know it now, this additional dozen number of finger breakings has already pushed the fragility that is her human hand over the bridge and into the realm of permanently damaged. When Artemis is sixty she won't be able to hold a cup of tea.

•

Artemis will be at home, alone, her husband long dead from something, and her hands will be so spoiled that it will be hard to open the refrigerator door. No one in her life at that point, including her daughter, will have any remembrance of the meaning attached to what it means to be a boxer. And the boxer part of Artemis will be long gone, too. She will have had four separate lives since the Daughters of America, not one of them involving boxing, and so her injury, these un-closable fists, will not be some battle relic, but, rather, a sorry, pathetic disability.

•

In the Daughters of America Cup every round is two minutes. There are eight rounds per match in this tournament. Artemis Victor hits Andi Taylor hard on the left side of Andi's head, throwing the round into ambiguity. It's the best punch that's landed. The bell rings and the judges stand and call the round for Artemis Victor and the two girls go sit in their separate corners.

•

As they sit on their stools, legs spread and red-faced, Artemis's and Andi's minds spin like wind turbines. The inside of both of their heads feels like rushing water. Their processing functions are working in overdrive. Sensory input has been delayed. Verbs are the only things that they can clearly hear.

•

Andi Taylor's thoughts travel in neuron buckets from her spine, up, in between her ears. In the bucket she sees her father, dead, watching television. His corpse is soaking up the blue rays of the light of the big screen. It's like her father is sucking at the void behind the screen of the television and the blue is streaming out of the screen, broadcasting into his corpse.

•

Artemis Victor's mind is a dull pink as she sits and thinks about her next move. Artemis Victor is like a battery that is recharging. All that skill, and practice, and physical Victor inheritance is building back up while she rests. She's going to come back into this round fresh, stronger than she started. Artemis Victor is going to hit Andi Taylor until she wins.

•

Get her, says Artemis Victor's coach to her. Hit her, Andi Taylor's coach says. Artemis and Andi, and all the girls of the Daughters of America tournament, wish their coaches weren't here with them, that they were allowed to fight each other without these embarrassing, know-nothing attachments. The coaches really are useless, like stoned older brothers getting paid by their parents to chaperone a middle school dance.

•

Outside of the ring are the two journalists and the other coaches and Bob and Mr and Mrs Victor and the other girls, who will be boxing later. The other girls are scattered in the vast warehouse of the gym. They're standing, staggered, not looking at each other. They don't talk to each other. They all look like separate witnesses. All of their arms are folded. They'll be in the ring soon enough, later today. There are four fights today. The other girls need to start worrying about how their own first rounds are going to start and end.

•

The Victor family teaches their daughters to visualize their winnings. Artemis Victor sees herself holding the Daughters of America Cup in her right hand above her head. She sees her left hand held up by the referee. Andi is nowhere. She's vanished. She evaporated when Artemis won the last round. There's one beam of light from the skylight and the beam is falling directly on Artemis. Artemis cradles the cup and shows it to her parents. In this vision there are people in the crowd who would have never come to one of Artemis's matches: girls from school who she competes for the same boys with, boys she'd like to sleep with, her older sisters, who rarely come see her fight.

This imagined winning in front of people who will never see her win, even if she does win, is symptomatic of the fact that Artemis Victor, like Andi Taylor, is, more than anything, delusional. Their desired audiences will never see them win. Even if they were to go and box professionally, hit some women in bikinis in the basement of a casino in Las Vegas, they wouldn't impress the people who they encounter in their lives outside of boxing. They would only impress each other: other women who are trying to touch someone with their fists.

•

Andi's mother doesn't even know what the Daughters of America Cup is. It seemed too complicated to Andi to explain to her little brother and her mother. They know she boxes at a local gym, mostly with boys, but they don't know that she is good at it, good enough to beat out a hundred other girls in the region to go fight in a state she's never before been in. Andi sits on the wood stool, waiting for the second round to begin, huffing like a maniac. She never was good with endurance sports, despite the fact that everyone always told her that her body would be good at them.

•

Nobody can ever possibly know what a specific body is good at unless they're inside it.

•

Sitting on her break stool, Andi sees her mother making her brother mac and cheese. Her brother is six. They don't have the same father. He's fine, the little brother.

•

There is a boy, a teenager Andi's age, another lifeguard at the community pool, who Andi really wants to make out with. She'd like him to be in the crowd at Bob's Boxing Palace. She did well the last round. Andi imagines him on the edge of his seat here in Reno. He'd be cheering, cringing at the near misses and yelling at her to keep hustling, keep swinging, keep hitting this Victor sister, the smallest of the Victors, in the ribs, where the hole in the air is. Andi will win this next round if she can find another vacancy. She sits on her corner stool, searching the air between her and Artemis Victor for a place in which she can put her fist. When Andi gets up she's sure she'll find a hole in which to hit Artemis.

•

The floor of the elevated boxing ring is a dirty caramel. The ropes that hug in Artemis and Andi are a red that has been bleached by the sun into a pretty pink. The walls of Bob's Boxing Palace are tin. The light from the skylight bounces off the walls and fills the whole space with a dull, dusty brightness. There are speed balls and hanging sandbags and lifting equipment in the corners. There is also a glass case that has dozens of belts and trophies and cups in it. Some are metal, but most are plastic. The big belts look like accessories from forgotten costumes. There are no plaques. If there are inscriptions on the belts or cups, they're hard to read because there isn't a display light. From far away the trophy case looks like a container of garbage and broken toys. One of the large plastic trophies, which is spray-painted in gold metallic, is flaking all over the floor of the case. The flakes look like gold confetti. The figure on the trophy, a six-inch-tall man in shorts, no shirt, and boxing gloves, has had most of his gold paint covering peeled off. Now the figure looks like a grey plastic toy soldier. There is a slit in the middle of the little man's head where the plastic mould must have come together.

•

Artemis and Andi move to the middle of the ring to start the second round. They bump fists.

•

Andi thinks of the boy she'd like to kiss from the community pool, how he's not here, how he's never been here, never will be here, how he saw her vomit after she pulled the red-truck kid's corn-dog leg from the depths of the pool on that sunny day. She had been wearing a red one-piece. All of the lifeguards had to wear red swimsuits. The women's one-pieces were close to a cherry. The men's swimming shorts were cheap and wrinkly, the kind you can buy in packs of five that fade quickly.

•

Andi had gripped the red-truck kid's leg too long. She thought he'd keep living if she never let go of him. The paramedics asked why she hadn't performed CPR. She hadn't pushed on his belly to get the water out from inside of him.

•

The classes the community pool makes you take to become a lifeguard happen over the course of one weekend in May. The trainers, who were also teenagers, had thrown a waist-up dummy, a nude-coloured half man without arms, into the deep end of the pool and told Andi to save it. The lifeguards hadn't even practised mouth-to-mouth. The dummy's mouth was just a ridge of plastic lips. There wasn't even a hole. Where was the hole in the air in which Andi Taylor could hit Artemis Victor using her fists?

•

Andi Taylor knows that, because of the rules, she has to hit Artemis Victor above Artemis's waistband. Andi hadn't felt much for Artemis in the first round. Artemis had just been a body that Andi was fighting. But now, they are two minutes in, and the direness of the fight has begun to become apparent. Andi drove twenty-eight hundred miles from Tampa, Florida, to get here. She spent all of her summer blood money. Andi's own mother barely looks at Andi. And here Andi is, in front of Artemis Victor. Artemis Victor has to see her. Andi is going to make Artemis Victor see her, and the next time Andi looks at Artemis, she begins to hate her.

•

Andi thinks wearing lip gloss is stupid, the way it makes girls' lips look sweaty and wet, and suddenly Andi is sure that Artemis has loads of lip gloss, a whole, sticky collection of lip gloss is definitely in Artemis Victor's backpack. What a stupid thing to like slathering on your lips.

•

Andi tried to find the vacancy again, the hole she had used to hit Artemis, but the hole was gone. Artemis had corrected her form between rounds. She was guarding her left ribs carefully. Artemis had a fortress of a body. The way she held her hands, up on either side of her cheeks, and her shoulders, slanted, and her stomach, tight and curled, made reaching her a near impossibility. Artemis practised two and a half hours a day, before and after school. She always did footwork and form correction in front of a mirror. She'd done it since she was young, half the height she is now. Artemis watched her sisters watch themselves in the gym mirror. Artemis had watched her sisters watch themselves since she was small. She saw how they had been able to make miniature corrections in the way their chests hung above their hips and the way they recovered from throwing all their weight in one direction to land a hit. Artemis and her sisters were each five years apart. They were like a Russian doll crescendo of sisters. They looked as if one could fit inside the other.

•

Artemis hated Andi, this sorry zit-ridden girl from god knows what part of the country. Artemis decided that as soon as she beat Andi she would see if there was any chance that the two of them could become friends. Artemis liked being friends with girl boxers, especially ones she'd beaten, because they all knew how good she was, how her family had a history of winning. Artemis was, after all, the crowned Victor, or would be, anyway, as soon as she got her fists to hit Andi Taylor's ears.

•

And then there it was, Artemis's glove right between Andi Taylor's eyeballs. Andi's nose bleeding. Andi's nose feeling like cornflakes. Andi swinging her arms like an idiot and Artemis sidestepping the space, where Andi is slugging, with an effortless grace. Andi looked drunk. Andi had recklessly killed that red-truck kid at the crowded community pool. Where had his mother been while the child was dying? Where was the babysitter when the kid's corn-dog leg went from alive to dead?

•

It's impossible to talk while you have a boxing mouth guard wrapped around your teeth. You have to spit it out to say anything, which is illegal, as spitting it out immediately stops the game and forces the spitter to forfeit the round in which they spit. Still, Artemis and Andi imagine themselves talking to each other. They imagine things the other says, and they imagine their own responses to their imaginary opposites, and so, above Andi's and Artemis's heads there are two different conversations taking place simultaneously. One conversation is Andi imagining Andi and Artemis speaking. And one conversation is Artemis imagining Artemis and Andi conversing. Both the conversations hang above each of their separate heads like a video game backstory scrolling through text.

•

Decades into the future Andi Taylor will not only not remember this imagined conversation, she won't remember anything about Artemis Victor's existence. Andi will, however, remember the tournament: how she drove four days and slept in her car to get there, how shitty and dusty the gym looked that she fought in, and the way the judges sat on the side of the ring, waiting to see her and her opponent touch each other, had sat like silent, motionless ghosts. They had been a panel of three. They were middle-aged men. All of their clothes were white. Even their white sneakers haunted Andi. They were balding and had bellies that hung over their white slacks. She watched them watching the other girls fight, in the later matches, after her fight was done. She was disgusted by them.

Andi will also remember the fact of that hole she was able to hit through to the other girl's ribs, but she won't remember the owner of the rib cage. Artemis will be gone from her. Andi won't remember Artemis's face, or her name, or the fact that Artemis had been a legacy, part of a family of prodigy boxer sisters, and that Andi had read several features on the sisters in the Women's Youth Boxing Association magazine and had even, embarrassingly, pinned a photo of the eldest Victor sister, Star Victor, above her bed before she ever knew she would one day fight the younger version of the eldest Victor sister. Andi didn't know then, when she pinned the picture, that she would, eventually, have hateful thoughts about the Victors, and an entire imagined conversation with the youngest Victor sister that she'd later completely forget.

In this way, decades into the future, boxing will be for Andi Taylor a kind of failed identity marker – something she tried on and wore around but that she later realised wasn't her, or didn't fit with the rest of her life, or her as a boxer didn't fit the way the world needed her to be in order for her to survive.

Not that Andi Taylor ended up desolate, on the side of a road, begging for water. She will become a pharmacist. She won't go to college at first, but then she'll go to community college later, and realise that she just wants to live a life where no one else is bearing down on her or threatening to die. She refuses to be the one who will find her mother's dead body. Her half brother will be old enough to do the body finding. Andi just wants enough money to have her own apartment, which is no small feat anywhere in this country, and so she'll climb the ladder of secondary education until she gets to pharmaceutical training, where she'll stop and think, This is a life I could live. I don't mind working windowless. The bright fluorescent lights and white coats of pharmacy life suit me. I can do this job and do it well. I've always had good attention to detail.

Andi Taylor has, in fact, always had good attention to detail if the detail is on paper. The details of her body, on the other hand, are harder for her to hem. She's never quite seen herself the way others seem to see her. Her outfits are poorly selected. She wears low-cut, flare jeans that are out of fashion. Her bangs, yes she still has them, are, still, awkward. Andi Taylor doesn't look in the mirror as much as Artemis Victor. Andi Taylor didn't look in the mirror as much as Artemis Victor when they were girls fighting in the Daughters of America tournament, and now, decades into the future, Andi Taylor is still bad at looking in the mirror, correcting what Andi sees of herself into how she wants to appear.

•

Watching yourself in the mirror was integral to the way the Victor sisters did their training. When Artemis Victor was sixteen her father had her start doing the speed ball in front of her reflection. At first she watched herself full-on. Artemis would let her eyes dart back and forth from what she was doing to what she saw of herself in her reflection. Looking at herself that hard made Artemis walk straighter, stand taller. It did wonders for her form. Artemis is able to self-correct her shoulders in minute increments. She knows the way her body feels when it is in the right position, and she knows the way her body feels when her form is poor, and so now, in this instant, in the ring at Bob's Boxing Palace, even without the mirrors, Artemis Victor is able to see her body from all sides, see the way she looks from above, below, and behind. Artemis Victor's body is a fine-tuned instrument. Artemis Victor will never have more control over anything than she does right now over her human form. Her muscles work like machines. These machines are about to unleash themselves on Andi Taylor. They're close to finishing her.

•

Andi is looking at Artemis with dread. Andi can tell something has changed in the way that Artemis is moving. Andi's nose is still dripping. Her blood is trickling into her mouth. The blood clings to her upper lip, in the dent in the centre, right below her nose. When this round ends, to curb the bleeding she'll have to stuff her nostril with a cotton ball soaked in synthetic adrenaline, basically the same stuff that is in an EpiPen.

•

It wasn't clear to Andi why the red-truck kid had been blue when she found him. Andi thinks about the game where kids dive for rings in the deep end. The rules usually go something like this: the leader has a clutch of diving rings that sink to the bottom when thrown in the water. The rings are a variety of colours. Sometimes they have numbers on them. There are usually between five and six rings. Many of the ring brands have inch-long white connectors that show where the ring begins and ends. The kid leader stands on the edge of the pool and turns around, their back facing the water. They hold all of the diving rings in one hand. On the count of ten they throw the rings over their head into the water behind them. Then a pack of children dives in after them. The kid who gets the most rings from the bottom of the pool wins.

•

Artemis Victor is sure that she is going to beat Andi Taylor. Artemis hits Andi again in the nose, and then the round is over.

•

Another round starts, and they keep circling each other.

•

Andi's only successes are because of the weirdness in the way that she holds her shoulders and because that weirdness is not something with which Artemis is familiar. But this weirdness in the way that Andi holds her shoulders is also a crutch, a deformed stance that opens Andi's body up to huge swaths of potential hitting. Andi leaves the whole left side of herself frequently unguarded because of her off-balance, off-kilter stance.

•

Because there are eight rounds per bout in the Daughters of America tournament there is the possibility of a draw. Even numbers will do that to you. There is also a point of no return, like in tennis. If Artemis wins five rounds in a row there is no chance of victory for her opponent.

•

The judges weigh the hits based on where they are on the body. The shoulder, the stomach, the rib, the arm, the ear, and the straight face are all weighed differently depending on the history of what damage the hit would cause if the opponent were hit there by a raw, ungloved fist. For instance, the ear: not only do you need it to hear but you also need it for balance. Without the drum you'll be horribly nauseous, your body unsure of whether you're on land or at sea, or being hung upside down with rope by your feet. In these Daughters of America matches, a hit on the ear is the highest hit you can earn because hitting a raw ear with a raw fist is the fastest way to kill someone. That and breaking their necks if you hit them hard enough straight on.

•

Artemis hits Andi Taylor in the ear twice and two minutes go by and this third round is over. Andi's initial rib-vacancy hitting seems forgotten and irrelevant these many minutes later. Her past pummelling doesn't even matter. Andi lost that round anyway. Her cornflake nose is dripping slowly. Her head feels hollow from Artemis's glove touching it. Andi doesn't want to lose this fight. Andi wants to fight the winner of the other match in her bracket. Andi wants another fight, needs another fight, so she can envision her little brother and mother watching her longer. Andi needs that imagined praise from them. She wants to watch her visions.

•

Regardless of whether Andi wins this match she will sleep in her car tonight. Most of the other girls are staying at a motel that has a pool, and a continental white-bread breakfast, but Andi already used all her summer blood money to drive to Reno and for the entry fee for the tournament. Alone, sitting in her car tonight, Andi won't think about the corn-dog-sized thigh or the way the blue of the TV screen had hit her father's dead body, like the blue was hugging him, or coming out of him, seeping out his pores. The blue had been underwater and metallic. Andi hadn't as much loved her father as needed him. She had needed another person in her life to tell her that she was a real person, and that she might not be special, but that she was fine.

•

Unlike how Andi's memory of this tournament will fade away from the centre of the way she remembers this time, Andi will remember the red-truck kid for the rest of her existence. She'll never be sure she didn't kill him. She'll see him, blue, at the bottom of every pool she'll go to for the rest of her life, which is why she'll quit lifeguarding and, within the year, stop wanting to make out with that boy lifeguard completely, because he was there, too, with the red-truck kid. The boy she wanted to make out with had watched her vomit. He had watched Andi empty herself of food and water and the apple snack she had eaten only moments before the drowning. The apple chunks in the vomit had been red and shiny, like bits of red plastic. She had been eating the apple while looking away across the pool, over the roof of the snack stand. She had been up on her lifeguard perch. To get up you had to turn your back to the pool and climb a ladder. The seat of the tower was a white plastic bucket of a chair. There was a red safety float she held over her lap and put behind her shoulders. She was supposed to throw it in the pool for someone to catch if she saw someone drowning. Someone, a mother who wasn't the mother of the red-truck kid, yelled, Drowning! And then there Andi had been, below the water, and then above it, with that nauseating blue corn dog gripped in her hand.

•

To be clear about the stakes: if Andi loses not only will she be out of the tournament, but this will be the last boxing match she'll ever engage in. If she loses today, this, hitting other women with her fists, will be over and closed off and become a period in her life that happened but that has been passed over, went through and gone and done.

•

Andi Taylor and Artemis Victor are facing each other. Andi Taylor starts rolling her fists in small circles. She's hitting the air mid-circle like one tests the temperature. Andi is hitting Artemis, not yet full blow, but tenderly, in different places to try and get a sense of where the hit will make Artemis's body go. It's a one-two technique where the advancing fighter hits their opponent to make them go one direction so that the second blow, the real blow, can hit them as they are moving in the direction of the second hit. If you did a one-two under somebody's chin it might kill them. That's why the girls' chins are tucked down and angled like flounder fish. Andi and Artemis only want to give each other the safe flat angle of their chins.

•

As Andi is circling her fists and prodding Artemis she realises that when she hits Artemis on her right shoulder, the rest of Artemis's body goes left and down, slightly. It's not a bad reaction to avoid a hit, but if Andi can smack Artemis on the left side of Artemis's head as Artemis's body falls to the left then Andi might be able to get in one blow, or two blows, or maybe even three, and then Andi has done it, is doing it, she's hit Artemis's right shoulder with her left fist and is doubling down on the left side of Artemis's head with her right fist. It's like Andi is driving a nail into a board with her right hand. Andi has hit Artemis's head two, three, four times, and then the referee gets between them and the round is over and the score is evened out a bit, 3–1. If Andi keeps on with her circling gloves she can dig herself out of this hole she's in. Andi knows she is capable of a comeback. Having a comeback would be better than beating Artemis straight out of the gate. Artemis is sitting on her stool, recovering. Andi is pacing, hitting her gloved fists together, keeping her body warm and ready to go back in and hit Artemis Victor.

•

Artemis's parents are yelling something at the white ghost judges about how could they let four hits in a row happen, the danger of it, this is a dangerous sport, don't they know that that's how people die? Mrs Victor is especially incensed. She's spraying words all over anyone in hearing distance.

•

Artemis is sitting on her stool. Her face is as red as her lipstick-clad, twenty-four-hour-durability-wear lips. Her waterproof mascara is smudged so it looks like she has the beginning of a black eye. Her chest is heaving up and down, taking in huge amounts of air and releasing that air back through her nose, oxygenating every cell in her mind. Artemis's tendons are tired and her head feels funky, like someone wrapped it in plastic and then pulled off the plastic bag quickly. Artemis's head feels hot. The wind, which is just the normal movement of air throughout the building, feels strong, almost as if it's blowing at her, almost as if there is a tube of air blowing directly onto Artemis's face.

•

This is the first time in her life when Artemis realises that she might be a failure. She is infuriated. Artemis Victor is a winner. This sorry excuse for a girl in front of her has embarrassed her.

•

Artemis looks at Andi's small hips and Andi's thin-tall strange tangle of a body. Andi doesn't know how to hold herself. Andi even breathes off balance, one side of her inflating before the other, so that Andi breathes a bit like an accordion moves, this kind of inflating and deflating side-to-side heave.

•

Artemis looks at Andi's hideous hair, its small, broken, split-end existence. Artemis thinks the worst thing she can muster about Andi Taylor: You are no one. No one will ever remember you. You'll die and then you'll be alone and forgotten and people won't have to pretend like you exist any more, they won't be forced to pretend that your existence matters because your body will be rotted and gone and no one will have to say that you are real.

•

The fifth round begins and Artemis is up hitting Andi Taylor, pummelling Andi's chest. Andi's body has become an object to Artemis, something that must be annihilated and dealt with. Artemis sees herself taking Andi's body and folding it into a cube. Artemis folds Andi's legs till Andi's feet reach Andi's forehead. Then she takes Andi's hips and doubles the body over, again, Andi's feet touching her forehead touching her hips. Artemis is sitting on the cube of Andi, Andi's young girl body now squashed into the building block of an object, and Artemis is pressing the block on all sides, shaping it like a carpenter, making the block smaller and smaller so that she can hold the cube that is now Andi in the palm of her hand.

•

Artemis is the type of person whose desires are so strong that she'll never forget them. If Artemis wants a thing, she does it, will do it, will perform any action to get the thing she wants in her hands. Artemis wants to win this fight for more reasons than the family legacy. Artemis thinks if she wins, if she's able to somehow beat her eldest sister, become the most fabled, the most brutal, the most beautiful of the Victor sisters, that a secret door will open for her, out into the world, away from her family, away from her mother, where Artemis has agency without her family that is greater than all the other types of agency she has previously known.

•

Artemis's parents are part of her identity. As in, she does have the teddy bear with the doll's shirt that says 'Victor'. However, Artemis resents this identity, too, or, rather, wants something more powerful that she can control herself, that she is able to make and look at and hold. And the fact of the matter is that the actual power that the Victor family has is extremely limited. It exists in small bubbles, in the very low number of women's youth boxing gyms that persist. In those spaces the name is fabled, but everywhere else – at the chain restaurant, at the department store, at the parent-teacher conference, at the real estate company where Mr Victor works – the Victors are close to no one. Mr Victor's numbers are down. Mr and Mrs Victor live in a double-mortgaged house in an undesirable suburb. They don't own any pets because pets are impractical and expensive.

•

The bell rings and Artemis Victor is advancing fast on Andi Taylor. Artemis is moving at a near run of a strut. Artemis's body is compact like a truck moving forward at a steady ten-miles-per-hour pace. It seems impossible that anything could ever stop Artemis's momentum forward. And then Artemis Victor's body runs straight into Andi Taylor's. It looks like Artemis is going to run her over, flatten Andi into a paper-thin pancake that will have to be peeled off the ground. Andi does fall but recovers in a kind of side stagger. Her left gloved hand catches her and she is able to use it to push herself back up so that she isn't ever actually exposed fully, lying on her back. In this way, Andi spins back up erect.

•

A tremendous dread fills Andi. How did she let herself get charged so thoroughly? How did she let herself get bowled over so flatly? The air around Andi feels gone, or thin, or in short supply. Andi feels weak and unable to see straight. Her eyes aren't working the way she needs them to. Her head feels as if it is filled with under-cooked pie.

•

In this moment Andi looks like a child. Something about her skin and the way it pulls around her eyes so tightly makes her look her age, which is seventeen. She and Artemis are both technically children, not yet able to join the military or have a drink of alcohol or have an abortion without the signature of someone who is related to them in most of the fifty states. And yet, this sport that they are playing, this simulation of killing, necessitates that Andi and Artemis understand themselves not as children, but as young humans, who possess the power to control their fate and their wins.

•

You can't train for a sport unless you believe you have control over your own destiny. The point of training is to change the outcome of the future. You train to change something you otherwise would have lost.

•

There is no debate that Artemis Victor has put in more training hours than Andi Taylor. Artemis has been at it for longer. She's honed her form for longer. Artemis spends more hours practising per week than Andi Taylor does in a month.

•

Andi Taylor thinks about the things that she's lost in her life. She thinks about her father and the way he made fun of her long arms. He called them tentacles because she was always grabbing for candy, or for his leg, or for someone to hold her, to scoop up her small body and hold on to it.

•

Andi thinks about her mother, how her mother doesn't really look at her, how her mother hasn't looked at her a lot since her mother had Andi's little half brother. She knows her mother loves her brother more because her mother likes Andi's little brother's father more than she ever liked Andi's father. Andi's father did things, Andi's mother said, bad things, and so Andi always felt she might have this badness inside her, though she wasn't sure exactly what that badness was. When her father was a blue corpse Andi couldn't help feeling that maybe she had made him blue in some way, or that the badness that her mother talked about had made him blue, or that she was blue, would be blue soon, because that badness that had been in him was in her, too. The red-truck kid's leg had been so blue, like all of his blood inside had been searching extra hard for oxygen. Andi had imagined his individual blood cells searching for air anywhere, pillaging it from his lungs, his heart, his toes, and his cheeks. Andi had lost the red-truck kid. She had seen him, alive, on the side of the pool, about to jump in for a ring. His goggles around his neck looked broken, like they didn't work at all. There had been a hole in one of the eyeball lenses. He was smiling, yelling at something. His vocabulary had been able to fit in a lunch box. Andi imagined all the words the red-truck kid knew in a single lunch pail, stacked in rows by his absent mother, forgotten at home by the babysitter. The babysitter would have to buy a lunch at the snack shack at the community pool.

•

How had Andi lost him? Andi was looking at Artemis. Artemis filled her entire vision. Bob's Boxing Palace and the ghost judges and the tin walls and the girls circled around the pink-rope ring that faded down into the ground, recessed fully out of view so that all Andi could see was Artemis, her smudged black eye and her thick hair and big, strong thighs that looked harder than any piece of stone Andi had ever seen.

•

Andi Taylor will be a pharmacist. She will have enough money to buy a piece of property. She will be loved by no one as thoroughly as her mother loved her younger half brother, and that will make Andi desperate and dogged for the entirety of her life. If desperation won boxing matches, Andi would be the victor by pounds and litres.

•

Artemis Victor hits Andi Taylor enough times in the ear and the head and the nose and the shoulder in this round to declare a victory five times over. The bell rings and the score is 5–1, which ends it there. There is no need for all of the rounds to be attempted. Artemis Victor has beaten Andi Taylor, which feels to everyone except Andi Taylor like what was inevitably going to happen. People are called underdogs for a reason.

•

Andi Taylor's body isn't as much tired as it is pulpy. Andi Taylor thinks of the way citrus fruit, if you peel back the bitter inner skin carefully, contains small, enclosed packets of juice. You can pop the small packets if you squeeze them softly in between your fingers. Andi's head feels like a bruised grapefruit. Why hadn't anyone taken enough care with her to give her some protective covering? A box, or a lunch pail she could have travelled in? How did Andi Taylor end up here, in Reno, Nevada, fighting girls for the right to hold a plastic cup? How did Andi Taylor end up so alone, so thoroughly beaten and made into pulp?

RACHEL DORICKO
VS.
KATE HEFFER

'Perhaps the future will not be like the past,' said Rachel Doricko, to no one in particular. Rachel Doricko had watched Artemis Victor destroy Andi Taylor. Rachel had stood with her arms crossed, watching from a corner. Rachel Doricko had thought that the ring looked like it had a sag in the middle of it until she got into the ring herself and was facing Kate Heffer, and it looked to Rachel now, sitting on a stool with her glove-clad hands in the corner, with her knees spread as wide as they could go, that the dead centre of the ring was a mound that might have one million bugs in it that, if you punctured it, would explode.

'I'm a toaster,' said Rachel, loud enough that the people in the crowd could hear her. Her mouth guard was in her right hand. She was hitting the top of her thigh with her fist, which had her mouth guard clenched in its grip.

Rachel had a theory about other humans: people are the most scared by what makes zero sense to them but that they cannot, no matter how they try, avoid. Because of this, Rachel tried to live her life in as frightening a way as possible, dressing like a man and an animal. She had a Daniel Boone–style raccoon hat that she wore everywhere, which worked quite well. It is amazing the power that a strange hat will give you.

And Kate Heffer was the perfect person on which to deploy the logic of the weird hat. Kate Heffer was definitely upset by weird hats. Rachel Doricko wished she could wear her weird hat now and spin it around so that the raccoon tail was in the front and she could put it in her mouth and chew on its rotten, tattered hide while staring at Kate Heffer from across this small expanse of a ring.

Rachel put her mouth guard in and banged her fists against her headgear. Kate Heffer looked at the gym, and the other girls in it, at the men referees, and the men coaches and the men judges and their sad paunches, and the few parents scattered about, applauding for something, applauding for anything, clapping seemingly only to applaud that the young women doing the fighting had bodies and could use their bodies for certain things, anything, really, which included boxing, which, to most of the parents, seemed like a funny coincidence, if nothing else.

It was midmorning and everyone had crossed that point in the day when they looked more awake than asleep and it seemed that the light in the gym was getting louder and louder and that here, in Reno, it would continue to get brighter and that this was just the tip.

Rachel Doricko and Kate Heffer had greater differences than the difference of their bodies. They each perceived time and understood the importance of their own lives in radically different ways.

Rachel Doricko was one child of many siblings and had the firm belief that there was nothing she could do to be significant to the world and that, win or lose, time would roll forward marked by arbitrary increments, and that was the only real thing she knew mattered and that she knew for sure.

Whereas Kate Heffer looked at her life and what lay before her and she allowed time and events to circle her, things occurring for the sole purpose that she could walk through them, be a part of them, and then move on. For Kate, time was a thing that existed only to have her in it. Kate was a goal setter. She made detailed lists and kept highly organised folders. She will become an event planner, making twenty weddings happen a summer, delighted by the fact that she has bent time to her will, orchestrated the event, and then the event has taken place.

Because of this, this match will be a series of events gone wrong for Kate, things she thought she could control but that get thrown back in her face. Rachel Doricko will take Kate Heffer's movements, one hit at a time, and pull them into herself and then spit them back out, better articulated and better made.

Rachel Doricko will count this fight in moments, in chunks of time that, in the hindsight of the match, glow with significance, whereas Kate will cling to the scoring system she's been given. Round after round, Kate will count and tally points.

Thus, for Rachel Doricko the bout starts like this: They are in a room. The room looks like a warehouse, but somebody has called it a palace. Everyone she can see looks like a conformist. The people stand separated from each other, nameless and lonely, with their arms folded. The people are down below, shorter than Rachel, not in the height of the ring, away from the spotlight of the fight and away from anything of importance that is about to unfold.

•

Three, one, four, thinks Kate Heffer. Kate Heffer thinks, One, five, nine, two, six, five. Kate Heffer is counting the ratio of a circle's circumference compared to its diameter. The predictability of the numbers helps her. She had to memorise the first fifty digits of pi for extra credit. Now the memorisation, with its sturdy sameness every time, is a comfort and a habit.

•

Rachel Doricko's weird-hat philosophy works excellently. Every time a hit is called, she sputters like an opera singer loosening her lips. The sound of the air smacking her lips together back and forth, pushing out of her mouth and into the ring, is startling. Rachel Doricko brings her forearm to her mouth in between rounds and blows on it. The sound the air makes as it escapes from the sides of her mouth, in between her arm and her face, is like an elephant.

•

Kate Heffer looks horrified. Bits of Kate's hair protrude out of her headgear and are stuck to the sides of her face.

Three, five, eight, nine, thinks Kate Heffer. Kate Heffer thinks, Seven, nine, three, two, three, eight.

•

For Rachel Doricko, the eight rounds of the match are organised by images, a basket of objects by which to remember the fight. Rachel uses the images like one uses mnemonic devices. She will remember the momentum of the match, where it was close and where she dominated, by the order of the images she remembers when she retells the story of her win in her mind. Her uncle taught her how to do this. He told her it was easier to remember images than words and that's why, if something is happening that she knows means a great deal to her, she must hang on to the brightest thing she sees, instant by instant, and then file the things she sees away in her memory of the day. She must remember specific objects from the moment, and then the remembered objects will become peepholes through which to access the entirety of her memory of the fight.

•

When Rachel remembers this fight in the future she'll think of these phrases in this order:

PLASTIC HAT
HUNDRED DOLLARS

WELL-FORMED INCREMENT
GOOD BOY
GOOD DOG
PENNY HOARDER
GOOD NIGHT

Kate Heffer, on the other hand, in this first round, is still counting her numbers. She is counting backwards and forwards, stabbing at time and the rhythm of her movements in the ring with a jagged, ill-constructed implement. Kate somehow knows that she is in over her head, that Rachel Doricko has better tools than her, but the momentum of the fight already has Kate Heffer in its grip, so it's too late, or Kate thinks it's too late, to change anything at this point.

•

Four, six, two, six, thinks Kate Heffer.

•

Everybody's hats are plastic, thinks Rachel Doricko. Look at them. All the cotton, everything that should be cotton, is really just woven melted plastic. You can see the particles of it if you look close enough. If I blowtorched that man's hat it'd melt instead of catching fire. The blue rim of it would drip in small puddles. Rachel thinks about all the clothes she owns spread out on the mat in front of her, all the basketball shorts and worn-down sneakers and ancient football championship T-shirts from her older brothers. Most of them are plastic, she thinks. Especially the jerseys. Rachel would like to spread out her clothes here, smatter them on the floor of Bob's Boxing Palace like she does in her own room. If her clothes melted on her body, thinks Rachel, which would be her least dangerous jersey? Which plastic pair of jersey shorts would do the least damage to her skin?

•

The plastic hat the man in the gym is wearing is on the head of a man who looks like a rich uncle. He looks like the kind of rich uncle who got rich on real estate or marrying the right woman, some type of wealth that requires no actual education. Or maybe no wealth requires education? thinks Rachel. Rachel is circling Kate Heffer like she is a wounded animal.

•

Fla! spits Rachel through her mouth guard. She's already landed enough hits to win a round. Kate Heffer can't keep herself together. Kate's planner, her notebook, her colour-coded reminders are long gone and out of reach in this endeavour.

•

Four, three, three, eight, thinks Kate Heffer.

•

Kate's gone into a panic and is losing badly. She looks weak and afraid. The judges and the onlookers can actually see the wince in her eyes when she sees the hit coming for her. Kate doesn't want to lose this match. Kate is trying to be the best at something. All Kate wants is to be the best at everything, and she feels that she has been tricked, or has somehow ended up striving for the wrong thing. Doesn't winning always count as winning? No, it doesn't, remembers Kate. Sometimes, Kate remembers, winning can be seen as threatening. What Kate wants out of the next sixteen minutes is not necessarily the win of a match, but the win of doing what she is supposed to do. Kate Heffer is a conformist. She's not good at asking questions. Part of this is based on the fear that things will go wrong if a question is asked, which has happened before, did happen before, could happen again. And so Kate is what's known as a people pleaser. Kate Heffer wants to please her parents. Kate will wear pink and smile ear to ear for every single picture. She never gets tired of taking family pictures.

•

But here Kate is now, in Reno, losing count, counting wrong, counting out of order. How did she get convinced to do something that she had the possibility of being bad at? How did she not know that this was a situation in which she would likely lose? Kate Heffer's mother once told her that girls grow up faster. Kate doesn't want growing up to be about losing. All Kate Heffer has is her ideas of winning. If there is one thing she knows, it's that being the best at something was supposed to be the dream. Rachel Doricko might be over there, spitting and crying and losing her mind, but Kate's got a lid on it. Kate will lose this match with a lid on it. Maybe, Kate thinks, if I keep counting backwards, keep doing the form I was taught and that I mastered, maybe if I just keep doing the same thing this fight will turn around. Maybe, Kate thinks, maybe this other girl, this sputtering octane valve, will give up, or burn out and die.

•

Three, two, seven, nine, thinks Kate Heffer. Kate Heffer thinks, Five, zero, two, eight, eight, four, one, nine.

•

Hundred-dollar bill, mutters Rachel Doricko incoherently through her mouth guard. Rachel can see it in her hands, the money pinned to the brim of her plastic trucker hat. It's prize money, but it's her own money. She saved it up and then cashed in the fives and the twenties for a single, crisp bill. She wanted to place a bet with one of her brothers that she'd win, but none of them would do it.

You're going to murder them, Rachel's eldest brother said. It is when he says things like that that she loves him.

Rachel has a horde of brothers who beat her. She has a love-hate relationship with the hits her brothers throw at her. On the love side it means that the brothers think of her as a boy, surely. Why else would they even talk to her? On the hate side, it means that she is picked on, and made fun of, constantly. Even the picking has some upswing, though. Rachel Doricko has thick skin and knows how to build her own worlds to live in. The world building has served her especially well. It was Rachel's eldest brother who found a gym for her in which she could properly practise. The excitement of it, as well as the fact that there were no women, made it an easy fit with Rachel's weird-hat philosophy, and so she took boxing up, and did it compulsively, both at the gym and with a bag she filled with sand and hung from a rafter in the barn.

•

Rachel Doricko's body is sinewy and scrawny. Her legs look like bundles of dry pasta covered in skin. Rachel's small for her weight class, and small in general. She's not short, but she is dense and thin-looking. She imagines her insides looking like pounded veal. Rachel laughs out loud when people call her pretty. It's always older or middle-aged women who say it. The women say it in the type of way that conveys that they have nothing else to offer – no specifics. It comes out ragged and awful, always, not because Rachel doesn't believe she is capable of some kind of beauty, but because she knows she doesn't have the beauty that these middle-aged women want, and that they are lying through their teeth.

•

It's not that Rachel Doricko has the right body for boxing. No Olympic coach would ever pick her body out of a line of bodies. Her shoulders hunch forward naturally. There is something awkward about the way she stands. She tends to blink more than necessary. Also, her hands shake, slightly. No one in her family ever thought to look into why that is. She just has shaky hands, Rachel's family thinks. Some people have moles on their faces. So what if their daughter has trouble holding a pen?

•

Kate Heffer, on the other hand, has the image of a perfect body for boxing. Everybody always told her so. In Seattle, where she came from, boxing seemed kind of edgy, like something she could do and talk about and that would make people think she was of interest and worth inviting to things and worth keeping around.

Everybody wasn't lying. Kate does have the body of a boxer. She's got thick, masculine shoulders and big biceps and no hips. She's always hated the way her body looked because that's what the pictures in the magazines told her. She thinks of herself as an embodiment of the term *bog-boned*, as in, she thinks of herself as having bones the size of swamplands. Only, her bones aren't bogs, or big even, it's just her arms and her neck and her head. She also has a Greek nose. Kate Heffer wanted to be a dancer, but with a body like that, nobody ever said, dancing, maybe that is a thing you should try.

•

That's the thing with children. So often what they do, or what they think they should do, or what they think they are good at is just some product of something someone told them that they would be good at. If you're tall people say, Surely you're magnificent at basketball. If you're a girl shaped like a block without hips, people say swimming, boxing, the discus, and then one thinks, Am I good at these things? Surely if people say it, it must be true.

•

Kate Heffer likes being good at things because she has delusions of grandeur. Kate Heffer imagines life-or-death scenarios where she is the only one with the right answer. Kate Heffer imagines herself saving everyone, everyone singing her praises, everyone crying. This is what will also make her an excellent wedding planner. She's a sucker for the pomp and a pump for the drama of event making. This is the most important day of your life, she'll say in the future. She loves saying those words to women and watching their eyes get wide. The women nod their heads in agreement. The women all agree that everything they've ever done in their lives has been leading up to this moment, which is exactly what Kate thinks now, circling Rachel Doricko. Kate thinks, Everything in my life has been leading up to this moment. This ability to believe that something as fickle and useless as time gone by has the human capability of intention is Kate's greatest hindrance, but also her greatest asset. Kate has the delusion of believing that events travel in a circle and that events circle her, which, while untrue, does lead to the competitive edge of entitlement. Kate deserves this hit, she deserves to land this hit, she deserves to win this round, and then she does.

•

Rachel Doricko is sweating like a madwoman, recuperating in the corner, mumbling to herself about how she wishes she could deploy her weird-hat philosophy – where is her weird hat? How did she ever agree to play a sport where they didn't let her wear her weird hat? Her headgear is itchy and hot and stuffy, like someone put an oven over her ears, and sometimes Rachel finds this stuffiness of the headgear comforting, but right now she wants to rip it off and rub her hands in her hair because she feels like there are bugs up there gnawing on her skin, running slip-and-slides in the rivers of sweat between her scalp and the foam-plastic that covers it.

•

Fuck, thinks Rachel, but it comes out as, Fla! The mouth guard makes her sound even crazier. If she loses, who will get Rachel's prize money? Who will get to own that crisp bill that is worth one hundred dollars? No one, thinks Rachel. She'll have to burn it. That's what it means to lose, thinks Rachel, burning something you've worked really hard for. You might as well incinerate it. Just light this match on fire and let it burn. It's always better to destroy something if you can't have it. Rachel Doricko plans to destroy Kate Heffer in well-formed increments. Rachel can hear Kate counting under her breath like she's a dancer. I'll take those numbers and ruin them, thinks Rachel. Let her count, thinks Rachel. Only people who don't know the meaning of time put on timers.

•

Seven, one, six, thinks Kate Heffer. Nine, three, nine. Kate's feet are moving in small circles.

•

Rachel Doricko hits Kate Heffer in the shoulder, then the mouth, and then the stomach. Rachel Doricko is building a mountain of hits. The structure of her hits is growing larger and larger. Rachel feels that she is winning in small, well-formed increments. Rachel watched a video of a man carrying a refrigerator up a hill on his back using a rope that went under the bottom of the refrigerator and was attached to a block of wood on his forehead. The man's back was at a forty-five-degree angle, bent to hold the weight that centred at his head. I'm pulling a refrigerator up a mountain using my head, thinks Rachel. My feet, they are going one in front of the other, thinks Rachel. I have this girl, this Kate Heffer, in a corner, thinks Rachel. I am going to throw her over the side of this cliff.

•

This is the way Rachel feels about accomplishments: they might be hard won, but ultimately they are meaningless. Rachel would never display a trophy, or tape track-and-field ribbons around her bed. Her brothers all do this, and she thinks it's foolish. What's the point in winning if you're just going to share the win with the viewer? Why taint the win by having to talk about it and show it off like a poodle? Better to win and just have everybody know it. Or, better yet, better to win and to have people talk about it when you're not present. Then you get to have your win in a place where your body isn't. What could be better than being whispered about when not in attendance? This is another reason why the weird-hat philosophy is something Rachel swears by. Give people something to confuse them, thinks Rachel. I've got this Kate in a place of confusion, thinks Rachel. I am going to beat her, thinks Rachel. Rachel feels like a thin veal cutlet. She's hot and overcooked. Rachel feels just thick enough that she might be able to wrap her body around Kate, smother her, and suffocate her. I'm juiced, thinks Rachel. I'm going to win this hundred-dollar fight.

•

Nine, three, seven, five, one, mumbles Kate Heffer. She's crying when they call the round for Rachel. All of Kate's control has oozed out of her. Her blood and her salty tears and slick sweat make it look like she is leaking pink Kool-Aid from her nostrils. Kate Heffer's Greek nose looks even Greeker. Her face looks flattened and red. It looks so flat that one of the onlookers down below the ring isn't sure it will ever recover. That does happen in these youth matches, doesn't it? Don't people get hurt so bad that their faces are permanently damaged? Don't people get damaged so bad that their injuries become lifelong souvenirs of a fight?

•

I'm a wildfire, thinks Rachel Doricko. Rachel Doricko has seen things burn to the ground before. She watched her childhood home go from there to gone in San Diego. She was so young when it burned to the ground that nobody believes that she remembers it. She was holding the hand of her oldest brother. She was six when the fire came, and they all had to pile in the family van. Someone knocked on their door in the middle of the night and said that there was a fire that was eating everything close by, and that this was the time to leave if you wanted to get out alive, so all the brothers, and her parents and her, the afterthought, got in the family van and drove to the ocean to camp on the beach and wait out the flames. It was two days of sitting in the sand and going to the grocery store for doughnuts and ready-made sandwiches. While they were driving away from the house she had turned her small head and looked over her shoulder and saw a flame licking the mountain behind her, the woods of her play falling into a black cloud of something, the line of the fire like an advancing army, moving slowly but steadily, in well-formed increments over the hill and towards her home. She was so young, the brothers said, there was no way she could have remembered anything. Nothing makes you believe that the world is meaningless like seeing things burn in a fire. A wolf kills a dog but doesn't eat it. A baby chokes on a piece of plastic. A deer gets hit by a car.

•

Rachel Doricko gets that this shit is meaningless. Win or lose this Daughters of America Cup, the biggest, most important, most competitive youth women's boxing championship, time will march on and Rachel will walk through it, and while there might be some meaning somewhere, it's not in the win, it's in the fact that Rachel is trying, the fact that Rachel is giving it her level best (her stomach tight, her biceps curled), and that is something that everyone can see, and even if they were to forget it, at least she would know that she made it here, to the best of the best of the nation, and she is winning, yes, absolutely, she is winning this fucking match.

•

In the crowd, watching this fight, is Rachel's grandmother, who drove Rachel from San Diego to Reno to get her here. Rachel doesn't have a car, so the grandmother was doing Rachel a great favour. Please, Rachel had begged, please drive me to this tournament. It had been easy for Rachel's grandmother to say yes, although Rachel's grandmother had not truly understood where it was that Rachel needed to go to. Rachel's grandmother has never seen a boxing match before, and is struck only by the dress, by the outfits and the gear and the headgear that the girls all strut around in as if they are crowns. So much confidence, thinks Rachel's grandmother. Everybody is so loud. The other girl boxers, the ones who are not currently in the ring, circle the bout like small fish watching a shark that has been trapped in an underwater cage. The girls watch the bout from a safe distance. Some have their headgear on but keep the chin strap unclipped. Others chew gum. One girl is balancing on one foot like a bird. What a strange thing, to have children, and to then have those children have children, thinks Rachel's grandmother. Where do their souls come from? Rachel's grandmother wonders as she watches Rachel slug her way through this match. As Rachel's grandmother thinks this, Rachel hits right, and then left, and then lands a hit on Kate Heffer's shoulder. Kate retreats and tries to remember her numbers. Zero, five, eight, thinks Kate Heffer. Kate Heffer thinks, Two, zero, nine.

•

An aerial view of Bob's Boxing Palace shows Rachel Doricko and Kate Heffer three feet away from each other. They've got their fists up in front of their faces. Rachel is rocking back and forth on her hind legs. Kate is moving her feet constantly, up and down, like a dancer. The onlookers – Rachel's grandmother, the parents, the two journalists, the coaches, and the judges with their sad paunches – are leaning in close. There is something unpredictable about the way both of these fighters move their bodies. They both look like their grip on the real has slid away. It looks like the squatter one, Kate Heffer, is counting, but they can't be sure because they can't hear or see the numbers coming out of her. Rachel makes loud sounds, grunts that have the shape of words, constantly. The sounds of Rachel's word shapes bounce off the tin of the warehouse-turned-gym. The sounds scatter along with the light into the ears of the other girls. The other girl competitors can hear the panting of Rachel Doricko and Kate Heffer. There is no music. There are too few people watching for the cheering to be deafening. Almost no one cheers and when they do it is loud and embarrassing – a single shout gone amok in this tin warehouse-turned-gym.

•

Everyone in the gym can hear Rachel Doricko's and Kate Heffer's bodies striving for the same thing. Bob's Boxing Palace is now so quiet that one can hear the sound of Kate Heffer's glove smacking Rachel Doricko's chest. *Thwack*, is the sound it makes. The thwack sounds like an open palm hitting a flat surface of water. Are both of these girls made out of water? The Reno heat is seeping up into everything. It's almost midday and everybody is baggy-eyed and sweating.

•

Andi Taylor, the sad, sorry sack of a girl who lost the last fight, is sleeping in her jalopy of a car outside the building. After her first-round fight turned into a go-home loss, she just wasn't sure she could look at any more faces. She'd looked at Artemis Victor's face for too long, though it had been a shorter match than Andi wanted. Andi's in snooze city because sleeping is her all-time best coping mechanism. She sleeps like some people drink liquor. Andi has slept off losses before, but she's never had to come down from so high up. The bout with Artemis Victor had been so high up that looking down felt like falling. I'll sleep off this loss, Andi thinks to herself. I'll sleep off the image of Artemis Victor pounding my chest. I don't need to see Rachel Doricko or Kate Heffer. One of them will win and then they'll fight a girl who isn't me. Either Rachel or Kate will win and then they'll fight the third Victor sister.

•

Artemis Victor is in the gym, under the tin roof, listening to the sound of Kate Heffer and Rachel Doricko breathing on each other. Rachel's got more hits, but not as many as she should have got by this point in the fight, and for how deep in the bout they are. At the beginning it seemed so clear to Artemis Victor that Rachel Doricko would be the winner, but now, with the heat creeping in, and Kate Heffer counting like she's about to detonate something, Artemis can't be sure.

•

Seven, four, nine, four, four, says Kate Heffer.

•

Rachel Doricko is trying to focus on filing the images in her mind that she plans to remember the fight by: the plastic hat, the well-formed increments of her piles of hits, and her hundred-dollar prize. This bout is not something that can be done over, thinks Rachel. There is no such thing as a rematch, unless you're famous, thinks Rachel. I can't let Kate Heffer creep up on me, thinks Rachel. I came all the way here to Reno for what, thinks Rachel. Rachel's grandmother looks at her phone to check the time.

•

The coach Rachel's San Diego gym sent to escort her to the tournament isn't even the normal coach she trains with. The normal coach Rachel trains with had another tournament, a seasonal, non-championship, men's tournament to attend. All the coaches Rachel has ever been trained by are men with something to prove, or something that's been lost. The coach Rachel Doricko has here in Reno has three kids he's lost complete custody of. Debt collectors plague his phone. He came to the gym Rachel trains at because he wanted a place to be in power. Rachel tolerates this desire of his like one tolerates a tax. Everything has a price, thinks Rachel. Everything I want I have to give something for, thinks Rachel. This coach has taught me things about form and stance but I have paid for it, thinks Rachel. The hundred-dollar prize money I saved should be mine, thinks Rachel. As she thinks this Rachel Doricko hits Kate Heffer again on Kate Heffer's shoulder. The hit is quick, like a jump rope whipping forward.

•

In San Diego Rachel runs long paths in the woods to forget where she is, what her body looks like, that she has a body that people talk to, that she knows how to talk. Running for Rachel turns into a hovering above her own head after the first two miles. It's good for the muscles, Rachel's regular coach from her hometown gym tells her. But really Rachel thinks running is best for forgetting she has a head.

•

Rachel can't get the image of her melted basketball shorts blowtorched to liquid out from under her eyeballs. She's looking at Kate Heffer, but has an imagining of burned clothes scattered all around her that is hard to shake off. Rachel remembers one specific thing from the fire. Rachel remembers her mother telling her to be a good girl. Rachel thinks this was an urging by her mother to get in the car, as in, Rachel, be a good girl and get in the car. They had to drive to get away from the fire.

•

What a sad thing, to be a good girl, thinks Rachel. God, how I hate the sound of it. Good girl, thinks Rachel, is mountains and mountains worse than good boy. All a good boy has to do to be good is put on a clean shirt. Nobody wants to be a good girl, thinks Rachel. There can't be a single girl in here who wants to be just fine.

•

Rachel Doricko wants to be amazing. She wants to be the wildfire equivalent of a girl boxing. Rachel Doricko wants the judges and the coaches and the other girls watching to look at her and see that she is advancing in the slow, steady, military line of a wildfire that is dooming Kate Heffer.

•

You're doomed, Rachel Doricko sputters through her mouth guard. Rachel's stomach is the image of a Roman suitor's. Rachel is a Roman boy who's been very good, so good she'll get a maiden, and in this instance, the maiden will be Kate Heffer, who she'll get to slaughter at will, if she wins this fight. The prize will be Rachel's to do with what she likes.

•

Fuck, says Rachel audibly through her mouth guard, but it comes out Phla! She's about to land a hit on Kate Heffer's stomach.

•

It's not that Rachel thinks being a boy is better than being a girl, or that Rachel wants to give up girlhood for boyhood, but that the words themselves (be a good girl) seem to her to perpetually be wearing a see-through jacket. Even when your mother is asking you to do her a favour (be a good girl) it sounds like she is asking you to wear a coat made out of clear plastic. How do words get like that? thinks Rachel. How do words become so gross and synthetic?

•

Good boy, says Rachel. Rachel tries extra hard to enunciate the *good boy* and Kate Heffer can hear the words through Rachel's mouth-guard-clad teeth.

•

Good boy? thinks Kate. What has Kate Heffer possibly done to deserve such an insult? Everyone in Kate's life says there is a place and a role for good girls, and Kate, you are a good girl, here are the rules of being a good girl and the instructions to follow for you to have a good girldom verified, and testified and confirmed.

We're all in agreeance, Kate Heffer imagines her mother saying. We're all inside the consensus that you're a good girl.

But will Kate Heffer be a good girl if she loses this fight? Perhaps this is the type of situation where losing counts as winning? Maybe if she lost, her parents would actually be happy that they wouldn't have to stay here in Reno to watch more of these fights.

•

Kate Heffer has put this fight on a pedestal. For months she thought that this was the moment that other moments would circle. She's logged her miles and counted her calories. She's memorised and then verbalised all the digits of pi that she has preserved in her memory. Kate Heffer has imagined her win, and the joy on her parents' faces. She thought the Daughters of America gym would be nicer. This gym is shit compared to her gym in Seattle. This gym doesn't even have window treatments. The skylights are unclean, which makes the light they let in look muffled and muted. The ring itself looks second-hand, or at least like something that has previously been flipped on Craigslist. What could you trade on Craigslist for a boxing ring? A really nice scooter, thinks Kate Heffer, or an outdoor, above-ground pool, or the labour it would take to paint many rooms.

•

Kate Heffer thinks she wants to win this fight, but with every passing moment she's less and less sure that a win would give her the glory that she wants it to. Is this a situation where winning counts as winning? Kate Heffer thinks of two famous female swimmers. The swimmers are number one and number two in the world, according to the internet, which Kate checks to be sure she's got the swimmers ranked right in her mind. The thing with these swimmers is that number two in the world is much more famous than number one on the planet. Number two (the loser) is on all the cereal boxes, and in all the sports commercials, and the advertisements for goggles, and even the charitable foundations that support young women use number two's face (the loser's face) to say they are doing good, big things in the world, and that their charitable foundation deserves money and attention and applause.

This, Kate Heffer thinks, is an example of how winning can count as losing. Unless number two in the world has won some other contest that Kate is not aware of? Perhaps this other contest does not involve swimming? Perhaps this other contest is about conformity to something, being a good girl in a certain way, saying the things you are supposed to say, and, above all, looking and talking the part of the role you've been assigned?

Winning doesn't always count as winning, thinks Kate Heffer with certainty, as she gets a point-earning hit delivered to her rib cage. One of her ribs pulls into itself. It goes up and in, slightly. Kate Heffer can feel her rib bending inward like a cheap utensil, the teeth of a plastic fork pulled in opposite directions. Kate Heffer suspects a magenta-coloured bruise will be left from her rib bending inward, but maybe she's wrong, maybe there won't be a purple flower, maybe her abdomen absorbed the pull her bended rib made against her muscles, and maybe she can hit back a little, maybe her parents can watch her, maybe she hasn't yet completely forfeited this fight.

•

The only thing worse than being a good girl is being a good dog, thinks Rachel Doricko. Rachel loves dogs, but she wouldn't want people to talk to her in that annoying, high-pitched whine. People say you're a good dog in the same voice they use to talk to children. At home, Rachel watches her mother's eyes get wide and Rachel watches her mother coo to the dog and say good dog and Rachel's mother shakes her head back and forth in front of the dog's face, as if to test the dog's ability to discern movement and attention and time.

•

Rachel hates fighting people who aren't desperate, which is why she is beginning to hate fighting Kate Heffer. There is no use in fighting someone who doesn't have their heart in it. Rachel's sick of this, and wants to end this match and make Kate Heffer cry. Look at her! thinks Rachel Doricko. Look at the way she's sad around the eyes!

•

Five, nine, two, three, zero, seven, thinks Kate Heffer. She's huffing through her nose.

•

One more punch, thinks Rachel Doricko. One more round and I'm going to get to watch Kate Heffer die.

•

Rachel Doricko's right arm is like a rubber band that has repeatedly been pulled back. It snaps onto Kate Heffer with loud, quick smacks. Kate winces when she is hit, but moves forward instead of back. Kate Heffer offers her face, with her hands limply in front of it, to Rachel Doricko like a poorly wrapped gift. Here, Kate Heffer is saying with her body language. My face, you can have it. Kate Heffer's coach, who, up until this point, has been quiet, is yelling at Kate to get her hands back up. Kate generally does what she is told, does what her coach tells her, but she's no longer interested in allowing the Daughters of America tournament to circle her.

•

The desire to please people is the desire to not be singular.

•

The first time Kate Heffer boxed it was because she had received an invitation. The invitation had come her freshman year of high school as a casual mention, from a girl Kate Heffer was hoping she could count as a friend. The girl who had offered the invitation came to a few sparring camps, but ultimately didn't stick around. Kate Heffer was left alone with the boys in the gym, which was a weird place for a girl to be, but at least it was a place where Kate Heffer could do a thing that she was told and do it fine.

•

While Kate Heffer's face gets hit by Rachel Doricko, Kate Heffer wonders if the girl who first invited her to box had liked her. Was Kate a person who someone might desire to have around all the time?

•

The crowd – which is not made up of fans but, instead, mostly of other participants in the tournament – can tell that Rachel Doricko is eating Kate Heffer. The room feels like Rachel Doricko is taking bites out of Kate Heffer's abdomen. There is a tenderness in Kate Heffer's annihilation.

•

The crowd can tell that Kate Heffer no longer believes that winning is always winning, and that this particular match has transitioned, in Kate Heffer's mind, from a must-win situation into an apathetic period of time, because somehow, miraculously, Kate Heffer has discerned, in the middle of this fight, that this moment, this match, which she thought was the moment around which other moments circled, actually has absolutely no meaning in her life.

•

The whole gym can smell this disintegration of Kate Heffer. Every parental onlooker and every boxer can tell that Kate is turning this fight into an event of non-importance. In Kate's personal priority of moments this fight is moving fast from pedestal to insignificance. Kate Heffer's mother, seated centre left on the back side of the ring, can feel this, and relaxes into herself a bit. She drove Kate from Seattle. She doesn't like boxing, and has had a hard time getting on board with Kate's competitions. But, with a squat body like Kate's (not to mention the Greek nose, Kate's mother thinks, so like her father's), all the normal rules about girls, and what they should be doing with their time, didn't seem to be a good thing, or an apt thing, to keep in mind.

•

I'm going to kill her, thinks Rachel Doricko. I'm going to kill Kate Heffer and watch her cry. Rachel pulls a one-two hit by faking right and then going left and then hitting Kate Heffer square in the eye. Kate Heffer's eye balloons and puffs out almost immediately. It's swelling faster than it should be. Keep going, Rachel Doricko thinks, I dare you, you fucking fat eyeball. Just swell up and shut yourself closed.

•

Rachel Doricko is about to hit Kate in the eye again, but then the round ends, and Rachel's left with time to pace in before she ends the fight. I counted pennies for this, thinks Rachel. I saved all my money for this, thinks Rachel.

How many pennies do you have? thinks Rachel. Rachel imagines putting a row of pennies, a whole roll of them, between Kate Heffer's teeth, and then forcing Kate's mouth guard out and making her spit it on the ground and making Kate chomp on the pennies until there is almost nothing left of Kate's teeth.

•

The oldest old-man judge is genuinely worried for Kate Heffer's safety. Rachel Doricko looks like a serial killer. Rachel Doricko looks like someone who is interested in grinding up Kate Heffer and making her into burgers.

•

Rachel Doricko and Kate Heffer no longer look like the same species. Rachel Doricko's eyes are wiggling from left to right across Kate's shoulders. Kate's face looks puffed and polluted with exploded red capillaries.

•

Rachel's pounded-veal legs are glistening. Sweat has pasted her hair to her temples. She's standing taller than Kate so her headgear looks grand, like the tallest building in a cityscape whose backdrop is the sea. Reno's midday light filters in through the skylight of Bob's Boxing Palace and sits on the heads of the onlookers. In their scattered chairs and leaning and standing poses, the onlookers look like court-of-law witnesses. Rachel Doricko wishes someone would interview them after. Did you see it? Rachel would ask them. Did you see Kate Heffer counting to nowhere? Did you hear that Rachel called Kate a good boy, and that neither of the girls wanted to be good dogs, and the way that Rachel made Kate chomp on pennies until all that was left in Kate Heffer's mouth was a hole of broken teeth?

•

Fla! Rachel Doricko says through her mouth guard. The last round begins and Rachel brainstorms ways to put Kate Heffer out of her misery. Kate Heffer is barely trying to move forward any more. She's just breathing loudly and shielding her face.

•

Kate Heffer's parents won't be sad that she lost the fight, even though they spent all this money, and came all this way, and took all this time off work to perform as supportive parents, cheering their daughter on to become the best at something, even though the thing that she was apparently suited to become the best at is questionable, at best. But with a Kate-looking girl, what can a parent do? Here she is now, being beat badly, with a puffed-out bloody eye that makes her look like her body is a single-use, disposable paper plate, and that the paper plate of Kate's body has been used for a barbecue where there is a lot of ketchup so that the ketchup has been dribbled all over the paper plate of Kate's face to such an extent that the plate is soggy and almost unrecognisable and most certainly no longer of use.

•

Kate's parents shout encouraging things like, You can do it, Kate! and, That's my girl! even though it is very clear to everyone that Kate is about to lose.

•

Rachel Doricko's grandmother says nothing. She is in simple awe of what she is watching.

•

In the end, when the last round finishes, and the referees call the fight for Rachel, and Kate's hit eye has puffed out to the size of a tennis ball, everyone, not least of all Kate Heffer, is incredibly relieved that the fight is over. The referee lifts Rachel's hand into the air. Rachel's eyes look around at all of the witnesses. She doesn't know anyone except her B-side coach and her grandmother, but now they all know who she is. Rachel's chest is heaving up and down dramatically. She goes back to her corner and sits down and spits out her mouth guard and starts to rip off the duct tape that holds her gloves on with her teeth. The ripping of the tape makes a loud sound in the tin gym, but it's drowned out by the witnesses talking and the preparation for the next match. It's lunchtime for the referees and the judges, so they leave their seats and go walk out of the gym to smoke cigarettes.

•

Kate Heffer has crawled out of the ring and is crying under the canopy of her parents. They shield her soggy body from Rachel's and the other girl fighters' vision. Kate knows that she is crying for her inability to become the best in the world at something. All her life, and all her lived experience, Kate saw time and events circle around her, for the sole purpose that these events could bring her forward to her desires. But now, here Kate is, bleeding, a desire clearly lost and not given to her upon her request, and so she completely reimagines the history of her own wanting, and decides that winning this match, that being the best in the world at boxing, was never something she truly wanted, but just a thing she was trying because other people told her she would be good at it. And later, when Kate is in the car with her father and her mother, driving back to Seattle, Kate will say this feeling to them. Kate Heffer will say to her parents, I never wanted to become the best in the world at boxing. And Kate Heffer's mother will affirm this delusional statement, this clear contradiction of what Kate herself had voiced only days before, and say, Of course you didn't, honey. Only vulgar girls become the best in the world at boxing.

It is this ability of Kate Heffer's to rewrite the reality of her own desires that will allow her to turn every narrative of her life into a self-fulfilling truth. She is, in this way, able to perceive and remember only those events that fit with her current perception of the world around her. Kate Heffer will train her brides from her wedding-planning business to employ this same strategy. This is the best day of your life, Kate Heffer will tell all her clients, and Kate Heffer's clients will look at her and reorder, and reimagine, and re-remember their desires until they are shuffled into the correct order that allows them to respond with confidence, Yes, this is the best day I ever had and ever will live.

The lot of them – Kate Heffer, Kate Heffer's supportive parents, and Kate's interactions with her future bride clients – drive off to a lavish meal at a restaurant of Kate's choosing to celebrate the end of the tournament for Kate, and thus provide her the reward she deserves, the reward she was always going to get, no matter what outcome actually took place. While it's not spoken about at lunch, everyone at the Heffer table knows that Kate will never again step in a boxing ring. Kate is old for her age bracket, and she has no intention of ageing into collegiate boxing, and this was really just something she was trying, not something serious, not something she really cared about, not something that she gave the power to hurt her, or show her a glimpse of her true self in any way.

•

Back at Bob's Boxing Palace the lunch break is ending. The witnesses are milling about and walking in circles. The sight of it, and the walking patterns of the witnesses, reminds Rachel Doricko of a coop of chickens. Because Kate left with her parents, there are even fewer onlookers than before. Maybe by the time we get to the second-round matches, Rachel thinks, it will just be the fighters and the people the fighters are thinking about in their heads. Rachel is eating an orange that she has peeled with her short fingernails. She's left her gym clothes on, but has changed her shoes to high-top sneakers and taken off her headgear and replaced it with her weird hat. Rachel feels that she's returned to a kind of home by again being able to deploy her weird-hat philosophy.

It's very hot in Reno, and it's very hot in the gym, so it would really make zero sense to anyone why Rachel would desire a Daniel Boone–style raccoon hat on her sweaty, recent-victory-winning head. The tail of the hat is facing backwards. Rachel is sweating heavily from the heat and the fight and the raccoon hair covering her ears and her neck. The sugar from the orange tastes incredible. Rachel wonders if it would be possible to pump herself full of orange juice intravenously. She'd love to have this orange go straight from her blood into her veal cutlet. She picks the white veins of orange peel gunk carefully off of each orange segment. No one looks at her as the gym prepares for the next fight. Rachel Doricko is alone with her win, eating her orange on the floor in the corner. Nobody says congratulations. Nobody says, What awesome perseverance. Her grandmother has stepped outside to get herself a bottle of water. Rachel thinks of herself as something people see but are unable to register. They saw her fight the match. She watched the witnesses watch her. But maybe instead of seeing a girl fight they just saw the steady small, incremental gains of a wildfire, Rachel moving over the mountain of Kate's body in a thick long black line over the course of the match, wearing Kate down, making Kate soggy, until Kate was just a burnt thing left in the debris, one of many, innumerable things that the fire had passed over, fundamentally changed from a living, breathing thing into the shell of a burnt trunk that crumbles to the touch and leaves black charcoal marks against any hand on which it rubs.

•

Rachel Doricko is still sitting on the floor in the corner when the end of lunch comes. From her line of sight, Rachel can see the girls who are getting ready for the next bout shuffle into order. The next-bout girls look like sisters. Both of them have long brown braids jutting out of their headgear. The referee walks over to them separately and checks for lead in each of their gloves. The referee puts his hands in one glove, then another. After the girls get their gloves taped on they look less like sisters. One stands straighter and one squats low, bent over. The bent-over one has a purple birthmark that starts under her nose and leaks down to her upper lip. The birthmark looks like ink pigment bled out over the lines of a colouring book picture.

Rachel Doricko loves watching people hit each other. She always makes a private bet with herself about who will win. She has her money on the girl with the bled-out purple lip. In front of Rachel Doricko, facing the ring, stands Artemis Victor. Artemis has fought both of these third-bout girls before. She fought them, separately, at regionals last summer. Rachel Doricko is still sitting in the corner of Bob's Boxing Palace, and is watching the back muscles of Artemis Victor, and Artemis is watching the third-bout girls bob up and down to warm up their legs. Artemis always watches how a fighter jumps and lands when they're warming up their feet. Everybody in the gym looks to the ring. The bell sounds and the first punch lands on the purple-lipped fighter. There are already so many point-earning hits in these first moments. It's clear that it's going to be a good match, so all nineteen of this match's witnesses, everybody outside the ring, stands up, folds their arms, walks towards the ring ropes, and huddles in.

IZZY LANG
VS.
IGGY LANG

In Douglas, Michigan, there is a town square with a statue of a dog that saved someone during a war. Iggy Lang wants to be a war hero. She would do anything to be a war hero, and to have a statue made for her in a park, too. Iggy would kill people, be killed by people, or turn her body into a dog's body just to have a statue of her in a town square that people passed and touched and looked at, and stopped and talked about, with affection and joy. Maybe I just want to be a dog, thinks Iggy. Iggy has, has always had, a purple stain on and above her lip, which already makes her look like a marked animal. Iggy thinks the spot is what saved her from liking people. Everyone else she knows is flat-minded and full of admiration for the television. Iggy just wants to be the best in the world at something, and Iggy is the best in the world at something. She is one of the best fifteen-year-olds in the world at boxing. She's got three more years before she ages up and out of this tournament, which means that by the time she is eighteen she'll be a reigning champion, because Iggy is going to win this fight, and the one after, and then she'll shape-shift into a 1940s spotted Labrador so that someone can make a statue of her and put it on a green.

•

The outside of Bob's Boxing Palace looks like Styrofoam, like you could sink your nails into it and chip off a little bit of the building and make the chipped-off bits blend in with a bowl of cottage cheese.

•

Adults, and people in general, are always telling Iggy why the fact that her face is stained purple doesn't matter, like it's some kind of impediment. She's never understood this. The thing she is self-conscious about is her crooked teeth. It's one of the reasons she started boxing. She saw her cousin, Izzy, fight a match and was jealous of her mouth guard. God, I would look good in that mouth guard, thought Iggy. The thought came to her one year ago, when she was fourteen.

•

The layout of Douglas, Michigan, is like anywhere, could be anywhere, which is how so many places feel to these girl boxers. They drive, or have their parents drive them, to far-out parts of the country that look like nowhere, and even the places that look like somewhere still have that Bob's Boxing Palace outside Styrofoam feel, with the facade taller than the actual roofing, and the malls with the Bass Pros, and the parking lots that swim for days, the parking lots that greet them at the tournaments they compete in, these runways of concrete, from their homes to these gyms in faraway states. The light does vary, some, and the way that the equipment feels, that varies, too, and the judges, where do they find them? Whose boyfriend of a sister are they attached to? The judges are same-faced but different every time. Men, all of them, who to the girls look uniformly ancient but are actually aged from twenty-six to fifty-five.

•

The magazine they all subscribe to, the magazine that you have to subscribe to in order to play, the WYBA, profiles gyms that have youth women's boxing programmes, but the profiles are always small with poorly reproduced photos. Iggy Lang remembers the first time that she saw Bob's Boxing Palace in a *WYBA* profile. She couldn't even tell what type of building she was looking at. It could have been a Walmart, or any other gym.

•

It's bad luck that Izzy and Iggy Lang are fighting each other in the first round. They've fought each other a million times before, of course, but this is Iggy's first Daughters of America tournament, and Izzy's second, being that Izzy is seventeen and Iggy is fifteen. What a thing, to have a younger kid-cousin boxer. Izzy hates her. Izzy hates Iggy's purple lip and the way she stares at everyone. Iggy Lang has no qualms about staring at anyone. Iggy Lang stares ablaze with her purple lip. Izzy hates how Iggy always keeps her mouth closed unless she has a mouth guard in it. When Iggy Lang has a mouth guard in her cheeks she smiles over it, purple lip curled over the red plastic, like a vein grasping at a side of meat.

•

Iggy and Izzy Lang look similar in the sense that they look like they were made from the same genetics, but Iggy has the purple lip, and Izzy is shorter, slightly, though Iggy boxes squatting lower. They both have a shared aptitude for muscle building. Their backs look like they have strings tucked under them. Their stomachs are quartered and squared and look like they've been made out of clay.

•

There is something about both Iggy and Izzy that is slightly ageless. It's the way their skin is pulled around their foreheads. The skin on their foreheads is tight, but sunbaked and wrinkled in places. Their creased foreheads make them look like they might be thirty, but their tight stomachs and arms and legs give them away for the children that they are.

•

Everybody looks ageless, or aged, or squashed and boxed in their red protective strap-on headgear. All the girls in the tournament feel this.

•

Izzy Lang hates the way that she looks in headgear. She can't wait to turn eighteen and age out of youth boxing and fight with a raw, unpadded head. Izzy has visions of knockouts. Izzy imagines giving and receiving knockouts. She imagines her vision narrowing in and her brain hitting the side of her skull so hard that her brain grows a flower, the bruise of it swelling, the light of the photographers flashing, saying, Shit, that Izzy Lang took one, and the photo of it, of the knockout, being in a magazine that regular people (not just girl boxers) read.

•

Twelve people are watching Iggy and Izzy Lang fight each other, four of which are other girl boxers. There are no photographers.

•

The light in Bob's Boxing Palace gives the pallor of Iggy and Izzy Lang's bout a topping of sequins. The warehouse's air is covered in dust, or maybe it's just that the light is so bright that it illuminates the dirt particles, making them into sparkly things that Iggy and Izzy punch through like bedazzled water, pushing aside the dust-light beams so their fists can touch each other's faces and ribs and cheeks.

•

Iggy idolizes Izzy. Iggy, the younger kid cousin, smitten enough with Izzy to follow her into the abyss of boxing. Both their names starting with I and ending with *y* and having double consonants that make them sound a little crazy. In Douglas, Michigan, there are only so many girls whose names make them sound a little crazy. How could Iggy not idolise Izzy, and why was Izzy so sad to have a kid-cousin follower? One would think that Izzy would have been happy to have a world co-conspirator, a boxing family legacy. Let Izzy win this year, and then Iggy can be her young successor, and inherit the jewels and the glory of her Daughters of America victory.

•

The hometown gym that Iggy and Izzy both box in reasoned that it takes only one coach to collect a cheque. Iggy and Izzy are sharing a coach in this first-round match. Their coach stands outside the ring, in a neutral corner. He looks like the relative everyone wished declined the obligatory invitation to Thanksgiving dinner.

•

In this Daughters of America bout Izzy wins the first two rounds and Iggy wins the next three. Iggy feels wild because of the run, and the judges and the referee have to tell her to sit down several times between rounds. Sit down, says the referee. Sit down, or you'll forfeit the next round.

•

Their glove-clad fists are touching each other. Iggy has a low, rotating swagger. Her braid smacks her back when she makes sudden movements, which she does frequently, as if trying to spook someone or say, Boo! It's the kind of aggressive push forward that dogs do when they play with one another. A quick run forward, and then a retreat, with a look in their eyes, over their shoulder, that says, Follow me, don't you want to follow me? That's what the quick movements are supposed to be: a goad for the other fighter, for Izzy, Iggy's cousin, to put her fist where Iggy pushes her body forward. Punch me, Iggy is saying with her goading lurch forward. Punch me here.

•

Iggy and Izzy Lang drove to this tournament together. They both sat in the back seat while Izzy's mother drove for twenty-nine hours. They slept in motels in North Platte, Nebraska, and Echo, Utah. In North Platte, after Izzy's mother was asleep, Iggy and Izzy snuck outside the motel to look for liquor. Neither of the girls was tired. They had slept all day in the car, filled with motion sickness and baked to sleep from the fast-moving, window-filtered sun. Izzy's mother looked dead while she was sleeping. Izzy's mother had walked into the room, crawled under the motel-plastic topper, turned away from Iggy and Izzy, towards the wall, and gone to sleep. The plastic topper had plastic decorative stitching. The pattern printed on the topper was a grainy computer graphic of a brown paisley. It looked like someone had searched for a paisley print online and then blown it up to the size of the bed. Izzy's mother looked like she was sleeping under a cheaply printed plastic poster. Izzy's mother's body looked like a plastic baggie filled with water. Izzy thought her mother's chin looked like chicken. The thought of having a body like that, of having a thin, permed head of hair, and a cookie dough neck, seemed impossible to Izzy. Izzy looked at her mother and saw a sleeping alien. Iggy looked at Izzy's sleeping mother and saw Izzy's mother sleeping. Iggy and Izzy walked out of the fluorescent motel foyer and onto the street. Their bodies were sleek tools slipping through North Platte. Iggy and Izzy could feel the clay of their quartered stomachs rub against the cotton of their oversized T-shirts and the waistbands of their tomboy boxer shorts. Iggy thought they could walk to the gas station and buy a beer, but when they got to the gas station it had been too quick a walk to get there, so they took a left turn down an unlit dirt lane so they could walk a little more and get the pent-up car juices out of their legs.

•

When Iggy had started boxing, and started following Izzy to the gym, Izzy had been annoyed, was still annoyed, by the tagalong attitude of her purple-lipped kid cousin. After Iggy started boxing, the boys at the Douglas, Michigan, gym, and the coaches, always lumped them together and said it was nice that finally Izzy had someone to train with, but Izzy had loved being the only girl in the gym, and she had loved fighting only boy boxers. She liked beating boys. But she also liked being beat by them. Iggy, in comparison, liked fighting the boys, but only when she beat them. If she lost, Iggy threw a fit. Iggy spit and cried after losing punches. Iggy sometimes threw her gloves at the floor, or at the heads of the boys who had just beaten her. When Iggy cried after a loss she stormed out of the gym and hit the metal wall, loudly, as she was leaving. Iggy made scenes, and it was unclear to Izzy whether Iggy enjoyed making scenes, or if Iggy couldn't help scene-making. Izzy was a cool, mellow fighter. And quieter. Because of this, all the coaches and the boy boxers liked Izzy better. Everybody likes a gracious loser.

•

On the dark dirt lane in North Platte, Iggy and Izzy walked slowly. Like siblings, they were both annoyed and comforted by each other. A warm summer wind moved behind them. Field mice scuttled at the edges of the road. The lane was flanked by the backyards of darkened houses. They were inside the spine of a neighbourhood. The unpaved lane on which they walked was supposed to be only for the homeowners to better access their garbage. The backyards of the homes had mostly metal chain-link fences. Up ahead they could see a few lights on in one or two houses. They felt like they were fish swimming away from Izzy's motel-sleeping mother, into the depths of the dark ocean, where they were so close to nowhere that they could have been anywhere at all.

•

Both Iggy and Izzy were annoyed when the head of the Douglas, Michigan, gym made them practise only against each other. There is no point in practising against the same person over and over. Iggy thought that practising against Izzy over and over was like watching endless amounts of crime television. Iggy got so bored that sometimes she got tired of beating Izzy and let Izzy win.

•

Kicking up dirt on the darkened neighbourhood lane in North Platte, Nebraska, the Douglas, Michigan, gym ten hours to the east of them, Bob's Boxing Palace Reno gym ahead of them, the combined collection of hours Iggy and Izzy have spent on earth counting in at under thirty-two years' time, Iggy and Izzy saw this summer, this long many-day drive from Douglas to Reno, as a turning point in which many, if not all, things would become defined. It was, is always, a big deal to traverse so many states, to be assigned to meet another you, an equal, another girl who lives in another world who also spends time alone hitting things with her hands.

•

The woman at the motel front desk had been sleeping. When Iggy and Izzy walked past her to begin their search for liquor-turned dirt lane meander, the woman at the front desk had looked drugged. Everybody looks drugged, thinks Iggy. Everybody looks tired or asleep. The woman at the front desk had hair that was blond and wiry. It had sizeable pouf. It was probably a nice pillow, thought Iggy. The woman at the front desk was sleeping facedown. In one hand she gripped a pack of cigarettes. Her other hand was splayed like a starfish. Her nails were purple talons. Her nails were nice, thought Iggy. Purple nails were a fun thing. Purple nails say, I'm here for the party. Maybe the front-desk lady had just been at a party? Maybe this is what going to a party looks like when you're older? I want to be older, thought Iggy. I want to be older and I want to be a champion and I want to have purple nails and a dog that licks my cheek.

•

Izzy is not only older, but she's also been boxing for longer. She's been building her boxing world – the world in which she is a boxer, and the world in which boxing can bring her glory – for two years. Since she began building this universe, she has made every decision in her life based on boxing: what time she wakes up, where she practises, where she works after she practises, the clothes she wears, the way she wears her hair, the notebooks she carries, the photos she hangs over her bed and the photos she sees when she wakes up and when she goes to sleep. Izzy's boxing self is folded into herself so deep, so buried in the folds of her, that it's unclear to anyone whether she'll ever let go of her boxing self and join the regular wheel of reality where nobody knows who's famous, nobody knows who's the best in the world at women's boxing, and certainly nobody knows who you, Izzy Lang, are.

•

In one year, Izzy Lang will move to Chicago, where she'll stay for the rest of her life. The drive from Douglas, Michigan, to Chicago, Illinois, is two and a half hours. It's a short drive, but a far-enough drive that it is clear that Izzy Lang left. When Izzy Lang is sixty, she'll do the drive three times a week to visit her ageing parents. By that point, Izzy Lang will be almost retired. She will spend most of her years working for the admissions department of a large university, doing the incalculable administrative tasks that an annual admissions process requires. She'll appreciate the predictability of it. Like a contractor examining a building well done, she'll revel in the orderliness of the students' applications neatly organised in boxes: accepted, waitlisted, rejected, confirmed.

Maybe Izzy Lang could have done something else, maybe Izzy Lang could have been an architect, or a contractor, or a plumber, but also maybe this was all she was ever going to do, and maybe being a career administrative assistant is just fine? Sometimes, in Chicago, when Izzy Lang walks to work, she walks by a boxing gym. Inside the gym there are often two young girl boxers. She always walks slowly when she walks by the gym, magnetised by what is inside. Looking inside will be like looking in a mirror she forgot she owned. When Izzy Lang is sixty and driving to Douglas to visit her ageing parents, Izzy Lang will tell her mother. Izzy Lang will remind her slumped-over, shaking mother, remember when I was a girl boxer? What did you think of Iggy and me trying to hit each other? You drove us so far at our request. How did you get time off work? Was there ever a time when you thought that maybe you could have been a young girl fighting someone with their fists?

•

I love fighting Izzy, thinks Iggy, mid-throw. I love the way she looks when I beat her. I love the way I feel when I beat her. It's the most important thing in the world to Iggy. Beating someone at something that matters more to them than anything is like squashing a fly. You can see the guts of a fly after it's been smashed.

•

In the world that Iggy has built for herself, Iggy and Izzy are locked in a familial battle for love and respect. They are fighting because they are equals, despite the fact that Izzy is two years older. In Iggy's world, she and Izzy might train for the Olympics together. Maybe they'll move into a house together, somewhere in Colorado, in one of those high-altitude endurance centres, where their blood can thin out and they can bulk up on oxygen together when they sleep. Iggy read about blood doping and would do it immediately if someone gave her the right instruments. She imagines her extra, oxygen-heavy blood being purple, like her lip. Everybody knows Iggy's purple lip is where she stores all of her power, like her ability to tell if her parents are lying to her, or if her older sister is high on something, or rain is due in a week's time. It's not like Iggy is a kid who thinks she can move objects around the room with her mind, she just knows that she has a way of seeing and of sensing that makes her better than other people. Iggy knows she isn't like most people, and that plenty of people think she is inferior. Most people in Douglas, Michigan, don't know her. Most people don't know that Douglas, Michigan, has a gym, and that in the gym there are girls, fourteen-, fifteen-, seventeen-year-old girls, fighting for the worlds they have built for themselves in it, in which their bodies are capable of projections of fear and power and legend. Iggy thinks the results of this fight in Reno will travel back to Douglas, Michigan. People Iggy knows and likes, and people Iggy knows and doesn't like, they will hear who won this match between these prodigy boxer small-town cousins. Surely the WYBA will, themselves, report on these equally matched but strange and fierce cousins? Iggy doesn't even care about winning as much as she cares about being seen as a legend, a part of a larger story that has a beginning, a middle, and an end.

The boxing world that Iggy has built for herself hangs in the room in Reno, above the bout, like a large circular discus. On top of Iggy's world is Izzy's, and on top of that, at the far reaches of the ceiling, are the worlds constructed by the other girl boxers. They pile up, one world after the other, like a stack of thin, scratched CDs. If you stand in the middle of the ring you can send your mind up through the hole of the worlds built by the other girl boxers. You can travel through the layers of different imagined futures, and the different ways each girl has of being. Artemis Victor's and Andi Taylor's worlds are the closest to the ceiling. They're smashed up to the skylight, their fight so long ago, earlier this morning, that they are a little hard to see. Andi's is splintering a bit, or scratched so bad that you can't tell if you're looking at a light refraction. Andi's discus of a world is covered by the boy who had the red-truck shorts on him, and images of Andi winning the match that she lost, which now seems so foolish. What a foolish thing, to think fighting in anything can save your mind from a witnessed tragedy. The boy, the red-truck kid, he's plastered all over the surface of Andi's worldview discus, which hangs in the air above Iggy's and Izzy's heads.

Artemis Victor's discus of a world hangs below Andi Taylor's. It's covered in photos of herself, photos of Artemis in dresses, Artemis on covers of magazines, Artemis with husbands, piles of husbands-in-waiting, telling Artemis that she is the very best, the only woman, the only thing, that they have ever imagined even looking at, let alone holding. One of the husbands from Artemis Victor's discus is reaching down and stroking the hair of an image of Kate Heffer, whose discus is directly below Artemis's. Kate Heffer's world is smooshed between the psyches of Artemis Victor and Rachel Doricko, in which Rachel Doricko's discus only depicts Rachel eating veal and wearing bare feet. Kate Heffer's discus is full of people and things that surround her. On one side of the world, Kate is looking up at a fish-eye view of the sky in which she can see all the stars that exist, even those behind planets. On another side of her discus, Kate stands in a room with thirty people surrounding her, looking at all sides of her and finding satisfaction in her presence and absolute expertise. Below her is the world of Rachel, the last membrane of a discus between the fighters who have fought previously in the day and the fighters who are fighting now, the fierce, equally matched cousins of legend, the Lang cousins. These fights, they move so fast and so slowly. For Rachel Doricko, bouts don't only stretch out time when she is fighting in them, they also stretch out time when she is watching them. Rachel watches Izzy and Iggy Lang move on each other like buckets of water being thrown at each other. They are made of the same thing, Iggy and Izzy Lang, and yet, somehow, made of nothing that is similar. It's not the purple lip, thinks Rachel. That is not what makes them different. It's the worlds that they've built to box in. It's the way they look at their own reflections. Rachel can see by the way that Iggy boxes that her ability to create a total, concrete world in which her being a boxer matters is stronger. There is one more first-round match after this, one more fight left over to end the day, and so Rachel looks away from Iggy's and Izzy's bodies for a moment and tries to see if she can see them: the two remaining yet-un-competed girl boxers. They're there, of course, as two of the twelve witnesses. Their world discuses, their understanding of themselves as girl boxers, are hovering above the floor, but under the ring's elevation. Iggy and Izzy Lang are dancing on them. Iggy and Izzy Lang are sandwiched between two sets of world discuses: the four that hover above their heads, the worlds of the girls who fought before them, and the two that hover under their feet, the worlds of the remaining pair, who will close down the gym for the night.

•

Walking on the late-night road in North Platte, Nebraska, Iggy and Izzy Lang hear the sound of an animal. It yelps a little. The wind carries the yelp to them and away from them like the yelper is moving both closer and farther away at the same time. Iggy and Izzy Lang walk towards the sound of the yelping. As they walk, the streetlamps' circles of yellow make them go in and out of spotlight. The yelping sounds louder. They exit one circle of light, and before they can enter another, they almost step on the yelper, a small boy maybe six or seven years their younger. What are you doing? says Izzy. Where is your mother?

•

One of Iggy's favourite things about fighting Izzy is that she knows Izzy will remember. Izzy's memory is a point of family swagger. Izzy's mother has Izzy memorise the grocery list before they go to the store and Izzy remembers. Izzy always knows who's ranked in what place and where the rankings come from. To fight Izzy, or to even be in front of her, is to be imprinted on her mind forever. Iggy loves this, and loves asking Izzy to remember. Izzy, remember the Easter when I climbed in the oven? Izzy, remember Grandmother? Remember her paper skin? Remember last Tuesday's practice? Remember Robert bleeding? Remember the family vacation where we saw the ocean and I called it the sea?

•

The afternoon light of Bob's Boxing Palace throws long shadows on the Lang cousins. Iggy Lang's face is mostly covered in shadow, so the two cousins look even more similar than before. Izzy's calves are flexed and split down the side by a long, defined muscle. Iggy is so covered in sudden afternoon shadow that it's hard to see where her body ends and the grey of the dusty shadow takes over. Iggy's tan limbs look like they are bleeding into the shadow. Then Iggy swings hard and lands several point-earning hits. Izzy will remember, thinks Iggy. Izzy will remember this hit, and the one after. I'm swinging hits straight into Izzy's memory, where the hits will live with the details of our shared family. Maybe it's a box, thinks Iggy. Maybe Izzy has a box inside of her where she'll put her memory of me beating her.

•

When the little North Platte boy was sure that he had been seen he stopped yelping and looked at them. Come into the light, he said. Why do you have that purple thing on your lip?

•

This little boy looks like a worm, thought Iggy. He had translucent blond hair that was shaved too close to his head, as if he had just recovered from lice or fleas. His mouth looked yellow and crusty. You look like a booger, said Iggy. The small crusty boy stuck out his tongue and then continued with his yelping. I think he's trying to be a dog, whispered Iggy. Iggy and Izzy walked away and turned left onto a wider road. I wouldn't mind being a dog, said Izzy. If you're a dog then you get older faster. Dogs are never really teenagers. They're just babies for a few months, and then adults for the rest of their lives until they get put to sleep. It seems civil, said Izzy, to not have to be a half thing, a half human, a.k.a. a teenager, for which things are so in-between for so long that it seems impossible to understand the way things really are.

•

Lying in the hotel room in North Platte, Nebraska, Izzy's mother wanders in and out of sleep. Izzy's mother wonders, with exasperation, why she was the one who had to drive Iggy and Izzy to the Daughters of America tournament. Wasn't she always the one doing all the driving for not only her children but also her brother's? Wasn't she the one who was always planning the family vacations? How did she end up the matriarch of not one, but two families? There is a saying that her mother always told her: Your son is your son until he marries his wife, but your daughter is your daughter for the rest of her life. Did her own mother feel that way about her? Izzy's mother doesn't feel that way about her daughter. Izzy's mother wants Izzy to feel that she is free to live without her. If Izzy wants to move to Chicago, Izzy's mother will not only let her, she will encourage her. Decades into the future, when Izzy's mother is dying, Izzy's mother will not regret this. Thank god, Izzy's mother will think right before she dies. Thank god Izzy has a life where she is more than this, more than just my daughter performing my every wish.

•

Was Izzy more than her mother's daughter? When she walks by the boxing gym on her way to work at the university, she can't help but wonder.

•

The thing about being down a round to your younger-kid purple-lipped cousin is that it looks bad to everyone. Izzy Lang is sitting inside herself in this sixth round feeling the bad look of the fact that now she has dug herself into needing a comeback. She can feel her shoulders shaking. Izzy can't tell whether she is shaking-crying or nervous-shaking. Iggy's wild lip and eyes are glued to her. Izzy's a better, more skilled fighter. Izzy advances forward, cornering Iggy into the rope of the ring, hitting her so many times that the round is over almost as soon as it began. In this round, Izzy lands hits in all the point-earning places. Izzy lands headshots and gutshots and armshots and ribshots and shots that curl up and then down like a knife making its way into a piece of cheese.

•

Iggy can feel the edges of her body blur into the shadow she inhabits. She has to make her way back into the shaft of afternoon light so that she can see more clearly the rounded outlines of her gloved hands. The next round begins and she shuffles into the centre of the ring, dragging her body towards her older cousin like one drags a wet rag forward. The trail of Iggy's physical form leaves a ghost of slime behind her. And then she is hitting her. Iggy sees her padded fists touch her cousin's shoulder. Even as she moves her hands, Iggy is still unclear about where her body ends and the rest of the world begins. She's so close to Izzy that she can almost see a bridge to her, a cluster of dust particles that seeps into her own skin and Izzy's skin at the same time. We're mixing together, thinks Iggy. We're cake batter. Iggy's hands are slow and measured. Touching Izzy takes almost no effort. It seems like the particles between them are pulling them together, urging Iggy to come closer. Iggy thinks if she gets any closer to Izzy she might be able to step inside her, place her body inside of Izzy's body so that she is wearing Izzy like a jacket. Izzy's regular lip draped over Iggy's purple stain. Izzy's two-years-older, slightly shorter body holding all their molecules within a single frame.

•

In crime television very specific things need to happen. There needs to be a body. Then there is a mystery. Then there is a false lead, and then the real one. Then the detective is implicated, or the crime is made personal. Then the guilty is identified, and is either punished or, because of bureaucratic bullshit, let free. Iggy feels that the only times she ever loses a match are because of bureaucracy. This is a sport that has a referee. The referees are stupid, but they are necessary. The sport cannot be played without them, and yet, they are always what keep the sport from being played fairly. Iggy imagines fighting

Izzy without a referee. She sees herself fighting Izzy outside of a time commitment, the two-minute rounds abandoned, the fight becoming a true matter of endurance, where speed, and one's ability to stay standing, are the only things that really matter, because if you're slow you'll get knocked over, and without someone to stop the other fighter, there you'll be, bureaucracy-free on the ground being hit so hard from above that it will seem like a miracle that anyone ever walked on two feet.

•

After they left the booger-boy yelper on the neighbourhood lane in North Platte they walked back to the motel immediately. They crawled into the queen bed opposite Izzy's mother and joined her in sleep. In the morning they woke up and sat in the back seat of the van while Izzy's mother drove another ten hours. The windows streaked endless rows of cornstalks. The corn was lined up in neat rows that, because they were driving so fast, blurred in and out of view. The blurred lines of the cornstalks looked like vibrating triangles. As soon as Iggy fixed her gaze on one line it merged into the other dozen that followed it. While looking at the rows of corn for hours and hours Iggy lets her mind forget what shape the lines are. It feels good to Iggy to look at something and know that what she's seeing is not the true shape of a thing. So many things in her life look like one thing but claim to be another. These rows probably really are triangles, thinks Iggy. Or, thinks Iggy, maybe the row extremists just refuse to admit that they are rows and triangles at the same time.

•

If this bout were crime television Iggy and Izzy would be at the point in the episode where the crime is made personal. This is not a random murder but, rather, a targeted, well-orchestrated trap laid for the detectives to become enmeshed in a much wider web of crime. The stakes are: whether or not Iggy loses she has three more years to correct the narrative and become the winner, but if Izzy loses, this is Izzy's last year aged in at the Daughters of America tournament, and Izzy will have to look in the mirror at that and fit that information into her identity as a boxer, and she won't be able to do it, Izzy won't be able to lose this match and also think she's a boxer, and it is at this point in the bout that Izzy realises this, and by realising this Izzy already begins to let her idea of herself as a boxer melt away. It's like Izzy is taking off a jacket. It's too hot in this shit gym to be wearing so much clothing. Iggy hits Izzy in the head so many times that the round is called immediately. Izzy had to make a comeback, and she didn't, so now she's left looking at her purple-lipped kid cousin who just snagged a victory. Iggy's huffing hysterically, blowing smoke out her nose, taking her mouth guard out and yelling at Izzy, yelling at Izzy about how stupid she is. Izzy! yells Iggy in the middle of the ring. You fucking idiot. *This was your tournament.*

•

Izzy's body is shining. There is a heat radiating off of her. Her sweat looks like oil. The afternoon light on her body leaves stripes of blinding white. The light is so bright that where the light hits her straight on it rejects the idea of her, Izzy's skin not being the colour of her skin any more but the absence of colour. And, because Izzy's greatest strength is her memory, she'll remember this moment perfectly. Izzy will remember Iggy crying and yelling, and the way it was so hard to see Iggy, hard to see anything, really, because the light had become so late and so slanted that it cut things out of the room.

•

Then the bout is finished and the sun sets below the window and the whole gym is thrown into a dark shadow. The twelve onlookers' eyes go dark from the sudden absence of light and nobody can really see. Then the overhead lights go on automatically. The overhead lights are large round fluorescent factory lights that have cages on the bottoms of them. When they click on, they have a ramp-up period, so they aren't immediately as bright as they are able to be. Izzy is still standing in the ring, oiled with sweat, knocked out of the tournament by her purple-lipped kid cousin. The fluorescent overhead lights are getting brighter and brighter. They're warming up, thinks Iggy, they're ramping up so they can hug the bodies of the last-bout boxers. The ramp-up of the lights makes a loud humming. Iggy and Izzy get out of the ring. As they're slipping their bodies in between the worn-out ropes, ducking their heads under and back up into the air outside the ring, Iggy begins to feel a sting at the back of her neck, like someone is pinching her skin with their thumb and index finger. Her nose hurts, even though Izzy never hit Iggy straight on. It feels like Iggy's body is pushing at the edges of itself, hunching and contracting and getting bigger. When Iggy jumps off the elevated ring, back onto the ground floor of the gym, she drops to all fours to do some stretching. Iggy arches her back and then pushes her spine to the ceiling. The knobs of Iggy's spine pop out in perfectly spaced small balls. Iggy's purple lip is pulsating. Iggy looks less like a dog and more like an alien, like some otherworldly being that isn't human, but is trying to trick a human into thinking they're human. This body, thinks Iggy, what a weird thing to live in. Iggy is still letting her win sink into the front of her forehead. Iggy hadn't really wanted to beat Izzy, but Iggy felt that Izzy had not provided a way for herself to not be beaten. When they drive back to Michigan Izzy's mother will play the radio so loud that they won't even need to talk to each other. These girls are as silent as recently divorced lovers, thinks Izzy's mother. Izzy will lie in the way back of the minivan, hogging a full row of three seats and sleeping with a towel covering her head. Iggy will be awake, hoping that underneath that towel Izzy is doing her family duty and committing the whole tournament to memory. Iggy wants Izzy to remember all the details of the fight, and what they ate for breakfast. Iggy wants Izzy to remember that this was Izzy's tournament, that everybody knew it, and that even Iggy, when they were done fighting, told her so, aloud, into the air for everyone to hear.

•

After the bout Izzy walks out of the gym as fast as she can to get new, gym-free air inside of her. In the gym she felt like she was huffing dust. Izzy isn't a crier. She's not going outside to weep.

•

Walking off the fight, Izzy passes other warehouses. She can see the desert mountains that overlook Reno standing in the distance. They look thirsty and brown. The waves of their backs are more smooth than craggy. Their texture looks close to beach rocks that have been pummelled until smooth and worn. Losing the fight to Iggy makes Izzy think of the time both their families went on vacation to San Francisco to see the ocean. The drive had taken so long from Douglas, Michigan. They were five and seven, decades away from each other in years measured by children, but still, somehow, Izzy had felt that Iggy had a leg up. Iggy's father and Izzy's mother were the ones who switched off driving. It had taken four days to get to California, and a fifth to get to the ocean. When they entered the city limits of San Francisco they went straight to the beach. Izzy's mother had wanted to take a nap, to check in to the motel they were staying in, but everyone else over-ruled her and said, Don't be ridiculous, we want to go put cold water on our feet. One of the many strange things about Douglas is that it self-identifies as a beach town. It cradles itself against Lake Michigan and is the town it is because of that lake. Because of this, Iggy and Izzy were particularly confused about what their parents meant when they said ocean. You cannot see to the other side of Lake Michigan, just as you cannot see Hawaii from a California beach. As they drove through the city of San Francisco it seemed impossible to Izzy that they would ever reach an ocean. How could something as big as an ocean be hiding so close to all these buildings? Finally the city thinned out a bit and gave way to mansions. Their family van climbed a steep hill where the blue of water filled their windowed vision, then the van pummelled down through a forested park and finally to a public parking lot where sand blew over the thick yellow lines that told cars where to park. Izzy was still small enough that, even in a booster seat, it was hard for her to see out the window. She had to careen her head, and push herself up, to see what was happening outside. Her mother pulled the door open and unlocked her from the vehicle. Iggy and Izzy ran towards the sand, which, from the parking lot, sloped down sharply. It was a hill of sand, and they fell down it and then got back up as they ran so that their descent down the sand dunes was a four-legged tumble in which they were running in parts, and then falling in parts, and then running down in parts again, quickening their descent as fast as they could so they could get to this, to this ocean, as fast as their small bodies would allow. Their parents trailed after them, but the parents were so far out of view and mind that, in Izzy's memory, they were simply not present. As Izzy neared the water she began to see that the ocean was violent. In her ears she heard the waves crashing, and as she ran closer, she realised that the waves were giant. Huge rock islands rose out of the water in the distance. They were sharp and serrated and white-tipped. The edges of the beach were equally sharp and jagged. The cove itself looked violent, like half of it had tipped over and spilled directly into the ocean, and like this other half might do the same at any time. The beaches of Douglas, Michigan, were nothing like this. The beaches of Douglas, Michigan, looked like bathwater. I've been raised on bathwater, thought Izzy. I can't believe that the small lapping of water I grew up with was ever described as a wave. This giant crash here on this California beach, that is what a wave is. That is how waves are painted. Waves that are made into paintings look like California waves because California waves are what Lake Michigan waves are imitating. Izzy walked closer to the water and saw that the water was foaming. The water left little ghosts of suds in the outline of where the wave had reached. Four of me could fit in that wave, thought Izzy, as she saw a wave rise and then crash down in front of her. Iggy had run up next to her. Iggy was hysterical with joy and breathless. They had driven in a car so long together. And now here they were, two cousins, seeing the ocean for the first time. It's the sea! said Iggy. Izzy didn't even know that there was another word for ocean. Izzy had thought Iggy said *see*, like, I see the ocean, which hadn't really made any sense at all. But then it was later, at the Marina Motel, when Izzy had realised that her much younger, weird and ugly, purple-lipped kid cousin just knew more. Something about Iggy's purple lip made her able to know more. Izzy was older, and was supposed to know more, but here Iggy was, already being able to see that a thing could be two things at the same time.

In Reno, Izzy watched the sun set over the tumbled-smooth mountains. I am the sun, thought Izzy, and my cousin is an animal. Iggy had always wanted to be an animal. Inside Bob's Boxing Palace Iggy was taking off her gloves and towelling her face dry so that she could watch the last first-round fight. The fluorescent lights of the night-time gym made the last two boxers of the day look like they were stage actors. Their gestures were slow and exaggerated. Their facial expressions seemed sinister and overacted. When the referee got into the ring to start the first round he looked like a hated magistrate trying to give a speech to the masses during a time of war. Neither of the last-bout girls looked at him. The last-bout girls looked only at each other. When the last-bout girls looked at each other the air in the room pulled into the chests of the witnesses. Iggy sat down on her heels and watched the match. This is crime television, thought Iggy. In crime television very specific things need to happen. These last-bout girls have to start with a body. Then there will be a mystery. Then there will be a false lead, and then a real one. And then, one of them will win.

ROSE MUELLER
VS.
TANYA MAW

In girls' hand-clapping games there are no winners. You may be chided for missing a beat, or for forgetting one of the lyrics, but there is no victory that lies ahead for just one of the participants. Hand-clapping games exist only in a state of play, or a state of rest. However, they are not free of competitiveness. There is a pressure exerted by young girls upon one another to continue to clap, to chant the tongue-tied lewd nursery rhymes for as long as possible. This competitiveness lies in the clapping pair's desire for maximum endurance. The lyrics of girls' hand-clapping games are endless. Their choruses always circle back on themselves so that the game is played on loop, begun again by the same lyric that signals the game's end.

•

As the referees begin this fourth bout, the last bout of the day, in this darkened warehouse where only nine onlookers remain, there is the implication of a loop, or the suggestion of a repetition, a circular groove within which the tournament has fit its narrative.

•

These last-bout fighters look caricatured in their desire to beat one another. They each wear frowns that make them look like actors.

•

The industrial bulbs of Bob's Boxing Palace cast omnipresent white like the lighting seen in theatres. In stage acting, makeup must be twice as caked to even show up to the eyes of the audience. Because of this, in this washed-out ring of light, Rose Mueller and Tanya Maw both look like they have monochrome white faces. Rose Mueller's hair is cut so short that you can barely see it under her headgear. Tanya Maw has woven her long hair into two looped braids. Her ovals of hair stick out of her headgear and place droopy circles on her back. Tanya Maw has her shoulders pulled forward over the centre of her spine. Tanya Maw pushes her hands towards Rose Mueller and Rose Mueller moves her own hands to greet them. They're not clapping, but their hands are smacking each other in rhythm. Tanya Maw can hear clapping rhymes as her fists touch the fists of Rose Mueller. I'm an actor, says Tanya Maw, in her head, to herself. Tanya Maw needs to play the part of the winner.

•

The most famous hand-clapping game Tanya Maw knows is the one about the tugboat, where the last line of every verse morphs from a normal word into a crude trick. Tanya Maw used to love this game, although now, at seventeen, she is decidedly too old to play it. There had been something wonderful about listening to even her best, most well-behaved classmates put words in their mouths that changed mid-breath from banal to naughty. The words had changed while still lodged in their throats. She could see the words themselves shape-shifting, the strangeness of the word *ask* changing into *ass*, a fly bug changing into a crotch-covering zipper. As a young girl, playing hand-clapping games for hours on end, Tanya Maw had seen small, one-inch sculptures of the morphing words on the tongues of her playmates. When her playmates got to the end of a verse, she could see the sculpture of the word re-mould itself from something boring into something forbidden, and then these forbidden word sculptures were spit out into a pile on the pavement between the two girls who were at play. The more verses the girls got through, the more forbidden word sculptures they made. In those early days of girlhood there were piles of these sculptures all over the playground. It was a graveyard of hand-clapping games that had been played earlier that day. Tanya Maw has never met Rose Mueller before, but the way that Rose is clenching on her mouth guard makes Tanya think Rose is about to spit out a forbidden word sculpture. There is something foul inside the mouth of Rose Mueller.

•

Tanya Maw and Rose Mueller are not hand clapping. They are boxing. But there is a collaboration in the way that they stand. When Tanya Maw extends her fist out Rose Mueller greets it. When Rose Mueller puts her left leg forward, Tanya Maw moves back. There is also, technically, the referee in the ring with them, but the referee is no one. The referee is less than a person. The referee and the coaches and the judges, they are all so deeply separate. They think they are involved with this game, that they have power, but Tanya Maw and Rose Mueller have hoarded all the power for themselves. What is going on between Tanya Maw and Rose Mueller has nothing to do with the judges. The referees and the coaches are like the teachers who supervise their breaks between classes. They exist only to tell one the rules of recess. They are never involved in the politics, in the colossal dramas that unfold in the minutes between classes.

•

Rose Mueller's and Tanya Maw's coaches do know each other. They have been coaching youth fighters who compete against one another for over ten years' time. They are not close friends, but they have already made plans to, later in the evening, go out together. They were both thrilled when the Daughters of America tournament announced that it would be at Bob's Boxing Palace in Reno. They are deeply excited for the free drinks at the casinos. Tanya Maw lands a hit that makes Rose Mueller's coach and Tanya Maw's coach shout. When Tanya Maw and Rose Mueller swivel the corners of their eyes to look at their coaches, they see the coaches' bodies with the faces blurred out.

•

When Tanya Maw looks at Rose Mueller she sees a girl with boyband hair and laser-beam eyes.

•

It can be intoxicating to play a sport that requires one to look in their opponent's eyes. Tanya Maw wonders, while staring into the eyes of Rose Mueller, if this is why she is interested in both boxing and acting. There are so few activities that allow the intimacy of staring.

•

When Rose Mueller looks into Tanya Maw's eyes she sees orbs that look like fogged-in planets. Tanya Maw has a stray speck of black outside the centre of her left eye. It's like a small piece of her pupil broke off and is orbiting a black moon. Rose Mueller thinks she sees the speck moving in a circle. Rose Mueller hits Tanya Maw in the ribs and the hit begins to turn Tanya Maw's ribs purple.

•

Rose Mueller grew up in Dallas. The playgrounds of her girlhood were littered throughout the various suburbs that satellite Dallas's strange neon core. On the Dallas playgrounds, Rose Mueller played the same hand-clapping games that Tanya Maw played growing up in Albuquerque, but some of the lyrics were slightly different, as if each group of clapping girls were connected by a thousand-mile-long tin can and string. Here, in Reno, Tanya Maw and Rose Mueller know each other, but they do not know that they share a clapping canon. Rose Mueller and Tanya

Maw are punching each other with speed and precision. Rose Mueller's short hair is fully wet. It is glued to her head. Rose Mueller's headgear and wet hair and head feel as if they are all made out of the same material. Rose Mueller imagines her whole body being made out of the plastic foam of her headgear. With time and sun, her foam plastic head splinters. In the beginning of this bout with Tanya Maw, Rose Mueller was sure that she could make Tanya Maw splinter. The sun, long set at this point, is of no help now. Tanya Maw and Rose Mueller are boxing under floodlights. Rose Mueller is pushing her fists backwards and forwards. She narrows her eyes towards Tanya. Tanya narrows her eyes back and returns the hit.

•

The invisible network through which young American girls learn hand-clapping games is fuelled by older sisters. The best older sisters from which to learn hand-clapping games are the ones who have recently departed from girlhood to driving. If one does not have an older sister, one must access an older sister through a friend. While it is from older sisters that the games are originally learned, once a game has been introduced to a group of girls it spreads among them like a sickness. If there is rumour of a new hand-clapping game, one must learn it as quickly as possible. If the new game (Lemonade Crunchy Ice, for instance) appears during lunch on a Tuesday, it must be learned by lunch on Thursday. In this way, a repertoire is built and enacted. The older sisters, while invaluable to the transmission of hand-clapping games, are also responsible for all of the mistakes in the lyrics. Their memories are not perfect. This is how whole states of girls develop alternate, new versions.

•

Decades into the future, Tanya Maw will, actually, become an actor. She will go to graduate school to learn how to fit her face into the faces of others.

•

There are hand-clapping games that can be played by more than two people. These games require young girls to stand, or sit cross-legged, in a circle. These games are closer to tag than to a dance. To begin the game one must touch two other girls' hands. Then, a rhyme is sung, a chain reaction of hand slapping begins, and the last person whose hand is slapped on the last beat of the rhyme must either run in a circle and catch someone – or leave. As these circular, multi-person hand-clapping games progress there are those still at play in the circle, and those who have been kicked out. The kicked-out girls may not re-enter until there is one girl who is left the winner. It is the winner who gets to decide when the game is begun again. In the Daughters of America tournament the game is begun again immediately when the tournament ends. The WYBA committee plans them two years ahead. The girl fighters already know where next year's Daughters of America tournament will be, and the one after. They are clapping each other out of the tournament only to be prepared to invite each other back in. Get out of the ring, Tanya Maw is thinking to Rose Mueller. Get out now – you can always get back in after I'm the winner.

•

In the first two rounds Rose Mueller and Tanya Maw split the wins. The nine onlookers left in the gym are rapt. By virtue of their presence they have a stake in the match.

•

Iggy Lang, Artemis Victor, and Rachel Doricko watch silently. They sit separately. The sound of the hits lands in their ears like rain droplets. The hits are loud and echoey and heavy.

•

As an actor, Tanya Maw will be given hundreds of roles to play. She will never be famous enough to not need other ways of getting money, but when she is old and frail, she'll become a beloved typecast granny. The granny roles will be easy for her because old people just get to say whatever everyone else is thinking. Like children and fools, grandmothers are not held to the same standards as the rest of society. They are given permission to wear their true feelings externally. The brutal honesty required of playing a granny is what makes Tanya Maw such an excellent granny actor. Her whole life she has felt it difficult to conceal her true feelings. And now, finally, at the end, she gets to become slightly famous just by making her face a transparent sheet. What she feels about the characters around her she gets to wear on her face at all times. Granny Tanya Maw never has to be kind.

•

Rose Mueller had a friend with a cat named Window. Here, in Bob's Boxing Palace, mid-bout, Rose Mueller imagines a window in the shape of a cat, and a pink rosebush in the shape of her own body. As Rose Mueller moves on Tanya Maw, to the right and then to the left, and to the left again, she sees her own legs morphing into flowers. Her arms become a tangled web of thorny rose vines, and at the end of her arm, where Rose Mueller's glove used to be, there is a pink bouquet. The bunch of flowers smashes into Tanya Maw's face.

•

In one of her granny roles Tanya Maw will play a widow who conspired to kill her husband at the same time as her best friend (also an old woman) conspired to kill her boyfriend. It will be a comedy that everyone knows. High school substitute history teachers will play it years after Tanya Maw is dead. It is thought to be a wholesome, funny narrative.

•

Rose Mueller will be dead before Tanya Maw's double-murder movie is ever made. Rose Mueller will be a villager, one of those people who dies within a mile of the place they were born. This is not to say that Rose Mueller is not, was not, capable of change. She has a steadiness about her. An uncanny idea of what to question, and what to accept. God, for instance, is something Rose Mueller struggles with. In Dallas, her village of life and then death, everyone she knew, including her family, including her hand-clapping girl-mates of yore, and including the man with whom she will eventually own a chain of weight-loss-marketed gyms, the lot of them believed in God in the way that one checks the weather forecast. There were crucifixes in every room Rose Mueller grew up in. Rose Mueller will remember the choreography of mass in her old age. The get up, sit down, get up, sit down, kneel, chant, stand up, sit down of all of it – the way the actions of the people in mass never seemed to have any correlation to the mass's song lyrics – these rote body movements are what Rose Mueller will remember as the truest, most pagan part of what God is. Rose Mueller was told during childhood that it is rude to ask questions. In mass, it was almost a relief to just be given instructions. But here, in Reno, as a seventeen-year-old crew-cut-clad girl boxer, there are no instructions. No one tells Rose Mueller to put her fist on Tanya Maw's shoulder. No one tells Rose Mueller to put her left hand up a little higher. And so, Tanya Maw hits her. The third round is called for Tanya Maw, and Rose Mueller and Tanya Maw go sit in their separate corners.

•

Learning to braid is also something that is generally taught by older sisters. Tanya Maw has a sister, although she is not here in Reno with her. Tanya Maw's sister taught her to braid, and taught her how to play clapping games with her hands. Tanya Maw's sister is two years older, the perfect age gap for wisdom transmission. On the large circular kilim rug that was in the flat, single-storey Albuquerque rancher they grew up in, Tanya

Maw's sister taught Tanya how to braid. Tanya Maw's sister took Tanya Maw's eight-year-old hands and separated her fingers. Tanya Maw's sister took Tanya Maw's hands and showed Tanya how to pull her hair in front of her shoulders, evenly on both sides, so that Tanya's hair was split directly down the middle and could be held in two clumps at the top of Tanya's spine. You have to start with pigtails, Tanya Maw's sister said to her. One of the motivations for teaching one's sister how to braid their own hair is to release yourself from the duty of sister hair braiding. The Ur-braid is a simple enough thing: three smaller strands woven together to make something flat and bigger. But, in addition to the Ur-braid, there are also fishtail braids, and French braids, and loop braids, and rope braids, and ladder braids, explained Tanya Maw's older sister. You can braid all of your hair, or just a few strands of it, explained Tanya Maw's sister. There are endless ways in which you can make your many smaller pieces of hair into something bigger.

•

The large circular kilim rug that was in the flat, single-storey Albuquerque rancher that Tanya Maw and her sister grew up in was the stage for countless instances of wisdom transmission. It was also the stage for family tragedy. It was on the rug that the sisters were told by their parents that one of their cousins had been crushed when playing in an old elevator. It was on the rug that the two sisters first heard their mother threaten to leave their father. And it was on the rug that the sisters watched the front door open, watched their mother turn the knob and spit on the floor directly in front of their father. It had been winter. Tanya Maw looked out the window and saw a trail of footprints in the snow that led to nowhere. There had to have been a car waiting for her mother. Let's braid each other's hair, said Tanya Maw's older sister. It is on the stage of the large circular kilim rug that Tanya Maw will first learn to fit her face into the faces of others.

•

For Tanya Maw, boxing will be something that comes later. A friend of a friend will take her to her first class. Boxing is better than being home alone with her father. School plays only happen twice a semester. Her older sister has also, by this point, left her, but not in the permanent way their mother left in winter.

•

It's not that all of the girls in the Daughters of America tournament are punching their way through a dead person. Tanya Maw's winter-disappeared mother, and Andi

Taylor's dead red-truck kid, are things that hover above these girls when they box, but they will also be things that follow these girls after. These disappeared people are part of these boxers. Like viruses, they are stored in their bodies, in the spaces between the vertebrae in their spines. Right when Tanya Maw thinks that her memory of her mother leaving her has disappeared, there it is again, in the front of her brain, in the space between her eyes. Boxing against Rose Mueller, Tanya Maw begins to think she sees the large circular kilim rug that was in the flat, single-storey Albuquerque rancher. It's in the gym, in a far corner. The red-blue colours of the rug change steadily as they weave from the centre to the border. On the rug sits Tanya Maw's older sister. She's kneeling with her legs parallel, with her butt touching her feet. Like Tanya Maw, Tanya Maw's older sister has her hair in two looped braids. Tanya Maw's sister is playing a hand-clapping game, but there is no one on the rug for her to play with, so she is clapping silently into the air, miming the movements, mouthing the naughty hand-clapping lyrics in a way that only Tanya Maw can see. Only Tanya Maw can hear the voice of her sister. Tanya Maw's sister loses her place in the hand-clapping game so she begins again. This fourth round is running out of time, the two minutes close to being finished. A red-lit digital clock on the judges' table counts down the last window for punches.

•

Like Andi Taylor, Tanya Maw drove herself to Reno. Tampa, Florida, is much farther than Albuquerque, New Mexico.

•

There is a small, kidney-bean-sized balloon inside every girl's head. The kidney bean is under the bone, above the nose, and between the eyes. Inside the kidney bean is a soup of everything that has happened to the girls in their lives. It is from the kidney bean that Tanya Maw sees the large circular kilim rug that was in the flat, single-storey Albuquerque rancher. A small reproduction of the rug, a rug the size of a flea, lives in the kidney bean in Tanya Maw's mind.

•

Inside Rose Mueller's kidney bean there are miniature crucifixes and barbells and strip malls and every neon sign in downtown Dallas. There are weight-loss programmes and her husband and her cousins. When Rose Mueller and Tanya Maw box, the kidney beans pulse and leak all over their minds. The large circular kilim rug that was in the flat, single-storey Albuquerque rancher bleeds in between Tanya Maw's eyes. Tanya Maw looks over and sees her sister still clapping the air in the corner. Tanya Maw hits Rose Mueller's shoulder. The round is called for Tanya Maw, which makes the bout 3–1 in Tanya Maw's favour. Those afternoons after school, the ones when there were no plays, those are the afternoons when Tanya Maw learned how to hit someone in the face, which is so different from learning to fit your face into the faces of others. Tanya Maw's right hand is good at hitting Rose Mueller, but her left hand is better. Tanya Maw knew she was a good actor when, after a performance, a stranger came up to her and said, 'You must have lost a sister. I have lost a sister. And I could see in your face, when Nicole loses her sister, that you, not you the actor, but you, had a sister taken from you. It has to be true.' Tanya Maw did not correct the audience member. 'Thank you,' Tanya Maw said. 'Thank you for seeing that I lost my sister.' The fifth round begins with Tanya Maw hitting Rose Mueller in the shoulder.

•

Tanya Maw and Rose Mueller are both vicious fighters. Their hits are ruthless and exacting. There is no pullback when they land a hit. The full force of their bodies leans into it. Their arms are strong, but their true strength can be seen most clearly in their legs. Their thighs are slick and wet, and, under the floodlights of Bob's Boxing Palace, they look less like the legs of a human and more like the legs of an animal. They're so close to each other that, from far away, from the corners of the gym, they look like two parts of the same animal, like four legs of a single body. The four legs stagger and lock and stagger and pull back and grunt and then separate and sit down. They are cleaved and then reunited in the fifth round.

•

Rachel Doricko watches this match while chewing on the raccoon tail of her Daniel Boone–style hat. She thinks the fighters are evenly matched, but that Rose Mueller's hits seem stronger. When Rose Mueller lands a hit Rachel Doricko thinks she can feel the quake of the hit up through her feet. Rachel Doricko's eyes are hot on Rose Mueller. If there are cracks in Rose Mueller's stance, they are escaping Rachel Doricko's eyes. Maybe, Rachel Doricko thinks, her feet are too wide?

•

Before each bout begins, the girls of the Daughters of America tournament do not speak to one another. Language has no place inside the gym. Inside the gym the language used is the language of animals – the language of smell and feeling and sound. Rose Mueller's gloved fist is a paw being pressed on Tanya Maw's chest. Rose Mueller's and Tanya Maw's fists greet and then retreat from one another. They are moving all over the ring with speed and vigour.

•

Inside Rose Mueller's kidney bean, in that small soup between her eyes, Rose Mueller stores her memory of every hand-clapping game she has learned in her life. This is also the place where Rose Mueller stores skills she's mastered so well that she has difficulty explaining how to execute them, and even, at times, forgets that she can do them. This is the place where she stores the strange choreography of mass, and the rules of card games, and this is also the place where her leaping left hook thrives. When Rose Mueller is older, still living in the suburbs of Dallas, still living as a villager in her village of life and then death, she will remember the leaping left hook that she mastered, and wonder if she still has it in her – does the leaping left hook, these many years later, still take up residence in her mind? And then, there it will be, out of her body and out in the world in the air. She'll be alone in the gym she owns with her husband, and the leaping left hook will surprise her. She'll summon it out of her body.

It will sprawl from her arm onto a body bag, and she'll look at it in awe. The way her legs will lift off the ground, hover above the floor, and stay, floating, while her left hand unfurls over and up – it is only while she is midair that she will remember that a leaping hook is sometimes called the hook of an animal. Like a gazelle who lifts all four legs off the ground when running, a leaping hook happens in between the time that one's feet lift off and then return to the ground. Rose Mueller's leaping left hook will be what finishes this round.

•

The gym that she will own with her husband, the weight-loss-marketed gym that Rose Mueller opened, it wasn't a passion project. It wasn't her trying to relive glory days or remember the time when she was one of the best in the world at boxing; it was simply a small business that she knew she could do. Like so many athletes who go from working out six hours a day to zero, after Rose Mueller stopped boxing, she gained loads of weight. It was then that she realised that she did not understand how to live in her body if she wasn't using her body full force every day. Her body had become a thing that she only knew how to throw at the wall or not at all, and then, with its years out of use, its years of sitting at a desk, her body was put out of order, her knees were in pain, and she could barely walk to her car. It is only then that Rose Mueller will ask herself if maybe there is a way to put her body back in order. She will remember the bench presses and the barbells and the dumbbells and the leg presses of her girlhood, but more than anything, she will remember the drive – the total abandon, and obsessiveness, with which she fought – the way that boxing overtook her life.

•

A life taken over can be wonderful. But it can also be sappy and stupid and dramatic. A play directed by God is many people's stage of choice.

•

Rose Mueller learned to say the rosary when she was eleven. The repetition, and the prayer lyrics, and the way you move your hands around the beads while you're speaking, all of it reminded Rose Mueller of games that involve hand clapping. The Hail Marys and the Our Fathers and the Glory Be all sounded so close to naughty song lyrics. In Reno, while she is boxing, she mouths the prayers and the hand-clapping rhymes in between rounds. It's just something mindless, something she can do without thinking with her mouth.

•

It's not that god is a bad thing to be obsessed with. It's just that when a group of people who believe in the same god come together things tend to tilt in particular, at times hateful ways. Rose Mueller is smart enough to sense this, though not smart enough to take up her own God-interest practice. It is difficult to send back a dinner after you have ordered it, especially in the suburbs of Dallas, and especially when you are a villager. In a village everyone knows everyone's business. In a village it's much, much easier to eat what you've been served.

•

In Bob's Boxing Palace, in this last bout of the day where no daylight remains, the floodlights make multiple shadows of Rose Mueller's and Tanya Maw's bodies. Each floodlight casts a different grey body onto the floor. The dozen grey bodies cast by the floodlights partially overlap with one another, so that at the centre of the bunch of shadows of each girl there is a dark core.

•

It was extremely easy for Tanya Maw to leave Albuquerque. Her father, yes, he still lives in the single-storey rancher, was not able to love anyone, including his daughters, after the departure of Tanya Maw's winter-disappeared mother. It is easy to leave a place that has nothing to offer.

•

Tanya Maw wishes her father was here in Reno with her. Tanya Maw drove to Reno from Albuquerque, New Mexico, alone. To get to Reno she had to drive through Las Vegas. When she arrived in Reno, Tanya Maw thought that Las Vegas, from the perspective of her car, had looked like one of Reno's parents. Was Las Vegas Reno's mother? If so, who was Reno's father? Reno's main drag looked like Las Vegas had shrunk its own glowing strip architecture and handed it down. The massive malls of Las Vegas were in Reno, just slightly smaller. The billboards for the cathouses in Reno looked older. The casinos in Reno looked the same as in Las Vegas, but in miniature, except for the large dome building in the centre of Reno, which has no Las Vegas predecessor. The large dome in the centre of Reno looks like a spaceship shaped like a moon. When Tanya Maw drove by the Reno strip to get to Bob's Boxing Palace, she slowed down. A marquee in front of the dome read 'Caesars Silver Legacy Resort and Casino'. I am in a place, thinks Tanya Maw, that named its architectural centrepiece after a Roman dictator who was assassinated by his own people.

•

When Tanya Maw is eighteen, she will move to Los Angeles. In Los Angeles she will try and fail and try and fail and try and succeed a little bit and then fail to become an actor, until the double-murder movie, when, finally, she'll become the beloved typecast granny. In the before times, however, in the years before her acting makes her money, she will act in a play where a mother leaves her daughters. Tanya Maw was always an acting extremist. She believed, fundamentally, that an actor need not experience a tragedy in order to act it, but then there she will be onstage, acting as her winter-disappeared mother, acting as a woman who has chosen to leave her daughters, and Tanya will know that she is not acting, but channelling something much, much stranger. In this play, Tanya will not just fit her face into the faces of others, she will fit her face into the face of her mother, and this acrobatic exercise will almost kill her.

•

The sixth round begins with Tanya Maw hitting Rose Mueller. Both of their faces look like the faces of actors.

•

The part came to Tanya Maw by accident. It was not a part she wished to play, but a part that was offered to her, and that she felt she couldn't refuse without losing face.

•

Tanya Maw hides her face behind her hands and moves her hands in small circles. Her looped braids are ropes that have been soaking in water. They slap against her back as she lunges forward.

•

Outside of Bob's Boxing Palace people gather in downtown Reno. Like moths to the light, they flock inside the casinos. The deeper the people go into the casinos the brighter the lights become, so that, at the centre of each casino, there is a white neon blitz. The people are like moths being lured to their own deaths, but instead of death all that awaits them are large, plastic, alcoholic slurpees. The slurpees are shaped like grenades. All the people suck on the straws and hold the grenades up in front of their faces.

•

Tanya Maw learned about the part, in the play where the mother left her daughters, from an old acting teacher. When she attended the first audition, she found out that, on recommendation, she had already been cast. She felt slightly sick because she knew that this was a community play that almost no one would attend, but she was drunk, still, had been drunk all her life with acting, and still felt that onstage, while trying to fit her face into the face of another, she was able to access a part of herself that no one could see. It was like the inside of her was so fragmented that it was only by acting, by consolidating her insides into the outward display of a fictional character, that she became whole, which is why this job of acting like her mother, this job of acting as a woman who had left her daughters, felt particularly terrible and awful to her, because this was not a role where she would be fitting her face into the face of another, but a role in which she would be fitting her face into the face of her mother. The drunkenness of acting, she wasn't sure it would come to her if she tried to portray her mother, instead of portraying something already inside her, and there was no way for her to understand if her mother was inside her. It seemed shocking, and implausible, that she could ever be inside her winter-disappeared mother. In the play, the mother leaves her daughters to be with another man. In the case of Tanya Maw's winter-disappeared mother, this is not what happened. Tanya Maw's mother left her and her older sister because she couldn't stand the single-storey Albuquerque rancher. The large circular kilim rug, and the unrenovated kitchen, and the toaster oven, and the yellow tile in the bathrooms, and the fake adobe facade, all of it had whispered something horrible to Tanya Maw's mother.

•

In the dead of night inside her mind Tanya Maw's mother visits her. When you don't have children, you can leave a place, explains Tanya Maw's mother. When you have children, if you want to leave a place, you must consider leaving the children behind.

•

Outside the Reno casinos is a walkway along the Truckee River where men flip prostitution calling cards at men passing by. The cards have fuzzy, 1980s-looking nudes on them, and numbers to 'the women's direct lines'. The card flippers slap the cards against one another to get the attention of the passers-by. The thrum of the flipping cards sounds like a buzzing cloud of bugs. To walk the Reno river walk is to walk a gauntlet of card slapping. The sound the cards make as they are slapped almost sounds like hands clapping. Some men take the cards and stick them in their pockets, while other men take the cards and then immediately throw them on the ground. In this way, the Reno river walk ground is littered with discarded Carlas and Emmas and Sarahs and Claudettes. Rosalias and Sophias and Olivias and Mias cover the ground. If you walk the gauntlet of card flippers and you do not look like a man, you will not have the cards slapped directly in your face, but the cards will still be slapped, just slapped out into the air in a more indiscriminate spray. If you're a woman and you try to make eye contact with the card flippers they won't look away.

•

Rose Mueller has honed the art of looking away as one of her key weapons. In mass, in work, anywhere in Dallas, really, her village of life and then death, she can get out of almost anything by looking the opposite direction. Here, in the ring in Reno, the look away does her a great service. Eye contact is the most subtle, the most effective form of manipulation that a fighter can possess. By looking at the ceiling Rose Mueller gives Tanya Maw nothing. Rose Mueller punches left and then lifts her eyes to the ceiling. She sees skylights filled with star-speckled black. At the bottom of her eyes Rose Mueller glimpses Tanya Maw pulling back, and standing to the side, foolishly opening up the right side of her body to Rose Mueller's fist, and then there Rose Mueller is, returned from on high down to the floor of the match, and Tanya Maw is, by this time, three hits behind, and huffing loudly. This sixth round is called for Rose Mueller, which evens the score, and effectively brings the fight back to zero. Rose Mueller observes her win and looks to her right and then to her left. She chugs water and sits down. She can feel the power in her body taking over her mind. Her chest and head and arms are hung perfectly on her spine.

•

Tanya Maw does not yet know that she will become an actor. Here, at the Daughters of America tournament, Tanya Maw is a fighter. But she is also just a child – just a girl waiting to see what her life will be like compared to the lives of the other people she knows.

•

In the play where Tanya Maw played her winter-disappeared mother, Tanya Maw felt herself blurring around the edges, blending into the scenery. In rehearsals she felt certain she was camouflaging with the set, disappearing into the props she held, her arms melting into everything she touched with her hands. It was something about acting out the worst thing that had ever happened to her that made her have to abandon her body. She delivered the lines word for word, perfectly, but stylistically horribly. It was her absolute worst performance. The director said she looked stiff, almost lifeless. Of course, Tanya Maw had thought to herself.

Of course I look lifeless. I'm just trying to be a thing instead of a daughter. The only way she got through the performances was by isolating herself for weeks before the play was staged and calling her older sister three times a day. The older sister would say, We're not there any more, Tanya. We're not on the rug any more, Tanya. But when Tanya Maw looked in the mirror, she could see the large circular kilim rug in her reflection behind her, and she knew for certain that she would, in part, live on the large circular kilim rug for the rest of her life. I'll die on this rug, thought Tanya. And she did die on that rug. Decades later she will pull into herself in the hospital, on those terrible sterile machines where everyone dies, and she'll feel what touches her hands, which will be at her side, and she'll feel the weave of the rug beneath her shoulders. Unlike most kilim rugs, this rug's weave was a braid – a braided rope spiralled around and sewn together to make something larger, like a snake curled into itself, or a cross section of the very centre of a flower. It's not so bad to have lived on this rug, Tanya Maw will say to her mother. It's a beautiful rug, Tanya Maw will say to her mother. When she left, Tanya Maw's mother wished she took the rug with her.

•

When the seventh round begins, Rose Mueller immediately hits Tanya Maw's ribs. It's not as strong a hit as Rose Mueller's leaping left hook, but it is point-earning. The judges call the hit and look at their phones to check the time. The suspense of the tied match is completely lost on the judges' dull minds. The judges have been judging all day. This is a Saturday, not a regular workday, because all of these judges do something else besides judging youth women's boxing. The judges work at Safeway and at Amazon fulfilment factories and inside the casinos with the alcoholic grenades. The white they all wear is not a uniform, but just a colour specification from Bob to make sure that they all look the part they are being paid to play. Some of the judges don't even like boxing. It was from YouTube videos, and a one sheet that Bob sent, that they learned about the game. The judges can't wait to get in their cars and drive to their duplexes, or go out and bartend, or go sit on a friend's couch and smoke weed until they pass out. The parents, and the coaches, and the piecemeal off-white, ramshackle chorus of men that the Daughters of America tournament has designated as judges, all of them are dull around the edges in a way that glares compared with the searing radiance of these girl fighters. The judges' armpit sweat stains look so earthly and sick, the clear mark of a human in decay, which is an aura that is completely absent from these girl fighters. These girl fighters are the opposite of humans in decay. They are accelerating away from death with speed and precision. Immortality wafts off of them. Even the dullest of the judges can feel that the girls are not quite human.

•

When Rose Mueller hits Tanya Maw on her face, and then again on the side of her head, and then on her arm and on her side again, Tanya Maw knows that the round will not end well for her. And then, the round has ended, and the round has not ended in Tanya Maw's favour. If Rose Mueller wins this next round, then this fight will be over.

•

Rose Mueller returns to God in a way different from the way that one takes the temperature. She's sceptical of a larger order, and sure that if God does exist, he doesn't have a body or a face. In Dallas, her village of life and then death, she goes to mass almost every day. The people in mass with her are what make her the least sure of God's existence. They are, most of them, cruel and small. In her weight-loss-marketed gym, she sees them in their workout clothes and observes their frail and failing bodies. Even the fit ones look slack and saggy. Their bodies had to come from somewhere, but she's not sure what to call the realm from which they came. Is a uterus the same as heaven? Rose Mueller thinks, while seated on a bench press. Here in Reno, the church chants are a comfort to her, although she's not sure why. Perhaps they're just a way for her to carry around the village of her life.

•

Rose Mueller was her current height, five foot ten, when she was nine. As a third grader, she looked like an adult with a child's mind. She was, and is still, a deeply quiet, interior person. Rose Mueller has always felt like it takes her at least two days to process anything that has happened. In the third grade, in her Catholic elementary school in Dallas, the other children taunted her relentlessly. Was it because of her size, and her unease at living in her large body? Or was it because she talked so infrequently? She was, by all accounts, heavily bullied. Shortly before the Christmas break of her third-grade year, she will find that a group of her classmates has, during recess, lured her into a sports equipment shed and then padlocked the door from the outside. She'll stay in the shed, trapped, until what feels like the end of time. Inside the shed, Rose Mueller's third-grade mind stretched out flat like the wide expanse of prairies that surround Dallas. Inside her mind she saw wind blowing the tall grass and, inside the grass, yellow wildflowers bobbing up and down. She saw the seasons accelerating and passing quickly. The prairies went from crystallised winter frost to verdant green spring to drought to death to sand in the blink of an eye. Her own body, Rose Mueller was aware, had turned to dust in her mind. When Rose Mueller was found, twelve hours later, by her parents and a group of teachers, she looked like a different child than the child who had gone to school earlier that day. When she enters high school, and starts boxing, Rose Mueller will think of her eternity in the shed and how the sun had set beneath the crack under the shed door like a bursting star. Boxing is the opposite of being alone on a dust-filled prairie. Rose Mueller loves every girl who agrees to fight against her because they have agreed to be with her without needing to speak to her. Rose Mueller loves Tanya Maw, even as Tanya Maw lands a hit on her. It is a gift to be alive, and to be fighting each other.

•

Much later in life, when Rose Mueller is an accountant, before she opens the weight-loss-marketed gym with her husband, she will develop a theory about children who were made to believe by other children that they might not deserve to be alive. Her theory is that in adulthood, these children become telepathic. It's as if the social failures of the past – one's inability to, as a child, navigate one's peers enough to escape torture – help hone a superpower of acute sensitivity to people over time. Rose Mueller will never be, never was, a talker, but she will often think she knows approximately what language is being spoken in other people's minds.

•

Here in Reno, Rose Mueller senses that Tanya Maw's thoughts are slow and viscous. When Rose Mueller hits Tanya Maw, Tanya Maw's limbs feel like thick white honey.

•

The most impressive thing about Rose Mueller's form is that she fights patiently.

•

Rose Mueller can tell that Tanya Maw is not fully here with her in Reno. Perhaps Tanya Maw has gone somewhere else in her mind?

•

As the eighth round begins, Tanya Maw tries to stop looking at her older sister. Tanya Maw's older sister is, still, to Tanya Maw's eyes, sitting on the large circular kilim rug in the corner.

•

Rose Mueller's father is here in Reno with her. He's a contractor, and it was difficult for him to find the time. Rose Mueller's father loves his daughter, his only child, although she is so silent. Rose Mueller's father doesn't think about the shed, or the fact that because of the shed incident, Rose had to move schools. Rose is older now. Now Rose is a teenager. She has friends, and does well in school, and her boxing coach says she boxes like a champion. I am proud of her, thinks Rose Mueller's father. Rose Mueller's father thinks this in the way that he commits to going to mass. It's not complicated, thinks Rose Mueller's father. It's not complicated to be sure that I love my daughter.

•

After Rose started going to public school, her parents still took her to the same parish where the shed incident happened, to go to weekly mass.

•

Tanya Maw thinks she can see something fragile inside Rose Mueller. Perhaps her bones, thinks Tanya Maw, are made out of glass.

Rose Mueller lands six hits quickly, and then this round, the last round, is over. Rose Mueller is the winner. Tanya Maw and Rose Mueller turn their backs on one another. They walk away from one another slowly, their shoulders hunched over. There is a panting and emptiness around. The onlookers are surprised that the day has come to a close. Rose Mueller and Tanya Maw were both such exacting fighters. They had moved together like they had been a part of the same animal. Perhaps, if the brackets were set up differently, they would have both advanced to the second round. Now that the first-round fights are over, Bob starts to talk to the judges and click off some of the overhead floodlights in the corners. Tanya Maw's corner vision of her older sister is plunged into black. Right before the corners of the gym go dark, Tanya Maw thinks she hears the slap of a clapping hand. Tanya Maw ducks out of the ring, takes off her gloves, and then walks over to Rose Mueller and shakes her hand. The judges are putting away the chairs for the night and cleaning up their trash. Despite the few people in the gym, the sounds the witnesses make shuffling across the floor and the sounds the judges make as they push in their chairs for the evening are deafening. When Rose

Mueller's and Tanya Maw's raw hands finally touch there is not the sound of hands clapping. Because of the other noise in the gym, when Rose Mueller's and Tanya Maw's hands touch, they hear nothing.

•

As the judges and the girl fighters and their parents and the coaches drive away from Bob's Boxing Palace, their headlights smear against the desert-encased roads. The earth on either side of the freeway is a red brown. Slide Mountain hangs over Reno like a crown.

NIGHT

Other people come to Reno to go to Aura Ultra Lounge, to go to Faces, to go to Splash and LEX and Dilligas Saloon. People want to go to Nelly's and Club Vanity. What Artemis Victor wouldn't do to be inside Club Vanity. If Artemis Victor were inside Club Vanity she would drink with a fake ID and mount one of the raised dancing platforms and dance until all of her clothes turned into water. Artemis Victor would dance until she, herself, was water. Artemis Victor wants the liquid version of herself to get sprayed all over the floor. On the night of July fourteenth, while the girl boxers sleep, Reno's clubs fill up with adults looking for a theme-park-style evening. There are quarters in the casinos' slot machines. The outfits the adults choose to wear out tonight are special. The twenty-four-hour lights of the casinos are like the lights in the reptile tanks at the zoo. They're always on and always hot and blue so that the insides of the clubs look like something other than day or night. It's as if, inside these Reno clubs, there is no sun and there is no moon. Inside the blue light the adults become their theme-park versions. Their skin looks better than it has ever been. Their bodies look slimmer than they are. Money runs through their fingers. They dance and drink and fuck with almost no effort. The adults wish they wanted anything as bad as these girl boxers want to be the best in the world at something. These girl boxers want to be the best in the world at boxing. The girl boxers sleep through the night. The girl boxers do not dream of clubs or casinos or dancing. On the night of July fourteenth even Artemis Victor dreams only of winning.

DEEP NIGHT

The stars that hang over Reno rotate like the sped-up view from an observatory window. In the centre of downtown, there is so much light pollution that it is difficult to see the stars. The closer one is to the Caesars Silver Legacy dome the dimmer the stars shine. The referee and the coaches and the judges and the *WYBA* journalist meet at Caesars Silver Legacy Resort and Casino to have a good time. While the girl boxers sleep, these administrators of the Daughters of America tournament drink. The coaches dissect the wins and losses of the day like vultures pecking at a dead stallion. If their girl boxer lost their match earlier in the day, they blame it on her failings, her inability to listen, her physical limitations. If their girl boxer won their boxing match today, they claim the win for themselves. The coaches of victorious fighters borrow their fighters' glory like slipping into someone else's luxurious dinner jacket. The coaches whose girl boxers lost complain about their wives and the mothers of their children. They linger over how nobody ever listens to them. Bob of Bob's Boxing Palace has no fighters in the tournament, so he is playing host. Shots are delivered on trays. He is thrilled by all the money he has made. Kate Heffer's coach is trying to sweet-talk the *WYBA* journalist. Maybe the *WYBA* journalist has some sway with the WYBA, and could the WYBA host the Daughters of America tournament in his gym in Seattle in a few years' time? The local Reno journalist, when invited to go out for drinks, declined. The coaches stay late and drink like fishes. The longer Kate Heffer's coach drinks the louder his voice is. Kate Heffer's coach laughs and smacks the other coaches' backs with his hand. They're hard smacks but inside the din of the casino the smacks are silent. The dinging sound of the slot machines being played is constant.

•

The moment the sun comes up nobody in Caesars Silver Legacy sees it. The parents of the girl boxers are, for the most part, asleep. Rachel Doricko and Rachel Doricko's grandmother are sharing a queen bed at the motel where the Daughters of America tournament recommended they stay. Rachel Doricko's grandmother is awake. She stares at the foam-tiled ceiling and then sits up and stares at the carpeted floor. When the sun comes up it is hot and bright through the motel blinds. When Rachel Doricko's grandmother walks outside on the balcony in this last moment of the night, she can see both the sun and the moon. In the distance, Rachel Doricko's grandmother can see downtown Reno and Caesars Silver Legacy Resort and Casino. The white-orb dome of Caesars looks like a barren ceramic planet. Rachel Doricko's grandmother wonders if people will ever live on other planets. It doesn't seem so far-fetched. Building a city in the desert seems like an equally impossible challenge, and here she is, with her girl-boxer granddaughter, at a youth women's boxing tournament, sleeping in what looks like uninhabitable land.

•

Looking at Rachel while she sleeps, Rachel Doricko's grandmother remembers the day she gave birth to

Rachel's mother. It had been a short labour. Rachel's mother had come into this world, and Rachel had come into this world, with very little drama. Maybe that's why Rachel has a flare for the dramatic, thinks Rachel Doricko's grandmother. Maybe she is making up for lost time. Maybe that's what the weird hat is all about. If there are aliens on other planets, Rachel Doricko's grandmother feels sure that they can't be any stranger than these girl boxers. Rachel's Daniel Boone–style raccoon hat is on the nightstand to the right of the bed. Rachel is sleeping with an XL Padres jersey pulled over her head. Before Rachel's grandmother tries to go back to sleep, she opens the Daughters of America tournament brochure to look at the tournament bracket. In the quickly shifting early morning light, the tournament bracket looks like a children's nursery mobile. The prongs of the bracket rotate, waver, and scramble.

JULY 15

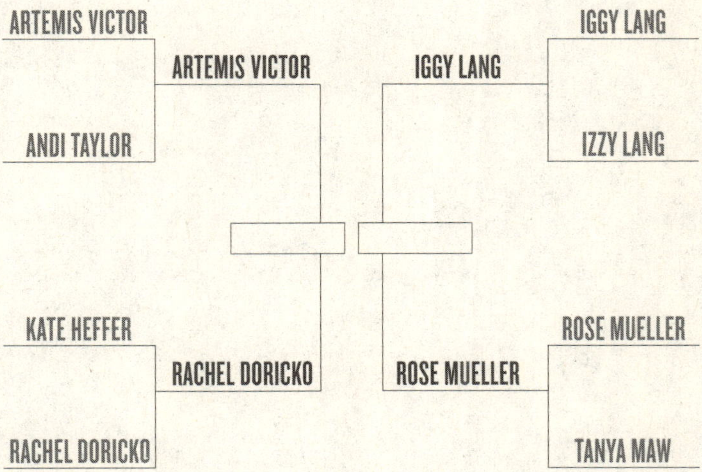
ARTEMIS VICTOR
ANDI TAYLOR
ARTEMIS VICTOR
KATE HEFFER
RACHEL DORICKO
RACHEL DORICKO
IGGY LANG
IZZY LANG
IGGY LANG
ROSE MUELLER
TANYA MAW
ROSE MUELLER

ARTEMIS VICTOR
VS.
RACHEL DORICKO

The continental breakfast served at the motel where the girl boxers stay is a graveyard of hard-boiled eggs. The spread is laid out in the lobby over a counter with purple laminate. There is watered-down coffee and miniature cereal boxes and bread that is so white that it looks like plastic. There are also apples, but the apples taste like sand. Produce stickers adorn the apples' too-red skins. The motel apples look like the apple Snow White ate before she fell asleep. The girl boxers who are left all went to bed early last night and slept the deep sleep of those much closer to birth than to death. The only things the girl boxers eat from the continental breakfast are the little individual tubs of peanut butter and the hard-boiled eggs. Rachel Doricko takes five of the tablespoon-sized tubs of peanut butter and four hard-boiled eggs. The hard-boiled eggs are served, sheathed in their shells, inside a warming clear plastic half dome that sweats. To open the dome, Rachel Doricko pushes the circular door up with her hands. To prepare her plate, Rachel Doricko peels each egg carefully. She opens each tub of peanut butter and puts the opened tubs in a line. Rachel Doricko makes three piles: a pile of eggshells, and a pile of miniature peanut butter tub wrappers, and a pile of peeled, ready-to-eat eggs. She eats the egg whites first, and then she eats the eggs' yellow, mealy centres. The last thing Rachel Doricko eats are the tubs of raw peanut butter. Rachel Doricko eats the peanut butter with her hands. Rachel Doricko dips her fingers into each tub and brings her fingers to her mouth. As she licks her fingers clean, Rachel Doricko looks around. Rachel Doricko hopes Artemis Victor is watching her, and Rachel Doricko hopes that Artemis Victor thinks that she looks like an animal. Rachel wants to seem as frightening as possible. In the small motel breakfast room that neighbours the lobby, Rachel sits and eats slowly. All breakfast, and the entire morning before the match, Rachel Doricko wears her weird Daniel Boone–style hat. The fur of the hat is old, and moth-eaten, and sometimes sheds. As Rachel walks off her breakfast, up and down the exterior stairs of the motel, and in circles in the parking lot, little clumps of her Daniel Boone–style hat fall to the ground. A trail of raccoon fur follows her into her grandmother's car, and into Bob's Boxing Palace. In Bob's Boxing Palace, Rachel Doricko changes from her weird hat and basketball shorts into her headgear and sports bra and snap-off pseudo-silk pants. Her mouth guard is clutched in her hand. Artemis Victor is already in the gym, sitting in a corner, talking with her parents. Artemis Victor never saw Rachel Doricko in her weird hat, which does not bode well to Rachel Doricko about how this fight will finish. One of the only tools that Rachel Doricko has against Artemis Victor is her weird-hat philosophy. Is Artemis Victor the type of person who would be disturbed by a hat that she doesn't understand? All Rachel Doricko knows is that Artemis Victor is definitely someone who cares about her appearance. Artemis Victor's hair is straightened. Artemis Victor woke up early to do her hair, even before a match. How stupid, Rachel Doricko thinks. What an insane thing to iron flat your hair's natural appearance. But straightening her hair is also proof that

Artemis Victor is a perfectionist. In many ways, Artemis Victor knows how to exist in this world in a way that Rachel Doricko, by nature of her weird-hat philosophy, can't. The weird-hat philosophy maintains that, by appearance, one announces themselves as a freak upon entrance. Whereas Artemis Victor can reveal herself to be a freak at any time. Looking at Artemis Victor, these last moments before their bout begins, Rachel Doricko realises that Artemis Victor is a stone mortar. Because Artemis Victor has given Rachel Doricko the flattened, straightened-hair version of herself, Rachel Doricko has no idea what is going on in Artemis Victor's mind. Artemis Victor could be the strong deep bowl in which Rachel Doricko will be ground into pulp. Artemis Victor is, after all, descended from her legacy of Victor sisters. Rachel Doricko has no sisters. The bell rings and they bump gloves. Did someone check that Artemis Victor's gloves didn't have lead in them? wonders Rachel Doricko. What if Artemis Victor's gloves have lead in them? wonders Rachel Doricko. This could be my last day on earth, thinks Rachel Doricko. Maybe I'll die in this ring, thinks Rachel Doricko. Rachel imagines Artemis Victor's leaded fist reaching her face and punching right through her eye and into her brain, and the centre of her brain becoming a bloody flower. Rachel Doricko imagines her body evaporating into an orange-scented mist upon death. Rachel Doricko punches right and then left. There is almost no one in the gym yet to witness the beginning of this second round. Bob and Rachel's and Artemis's coaches and the judges are barely awake enough yet to even process what about the way that Artemis Victor is boxing is unsound.

•

Artemis Victor thinks of herself not as a stone mortar but as a bucket of water. Anybody who has ever seen a flood knows the violence that water can do. But water can also be violent in a smaller, more insidious fashion. The smallest leak in a pipe can destroy a house from the inside out. One time, Artemis Victor was house-sitting for a neighbour who was gone for the winter, just coming by once a week to water their plants, and one week, when Artemis Victor came to the house, she realised that the house looked like it was sagging. The frames around the windows were bent, bloated with water, and curling away from the house. When Artemis Victor opened the front door, she saw that paint was peeling off the walls and water was dripping out of all the light fixtures. The first-floor ceiling of the house bowed and looked like it was going to collapse. People say hell is made of fire, but to Artemis Victor, hell looks like water. Artemis Victor wants to fight Rachel Doricko with a ruthless, relentless drip. It will be water that destroys the world's last handwritten scripts.

•

Rachel Doricko's body is a fraction of Artemis Victor's. Even though they are in the same weight class, here in the ring, Artemis Victor looks twice as thick. Artemis Victor's body is a toned cut of meat, whereas Rachel Doricko's body is a thin smashed cutlet. Rachel Doricko's body looks like it's been flattened, like its density has been compacted and her muscle has been forced to fit into a skin that's too small. In the first and second rounds, Artemis Victor wins quickly, like a mother putting away toys at the end of the day. But the third round gets wild and throws the fight out into space. In the third round, Rachel Doricko starts doing something funny with her legs. Rachel Doricko weaves and side-steps her feet like someone learning how to dance. The weirdness of it makes Artemis Victor lose her position. And then there Rachel Doricko is, at Artemis Victor's shoulder. Artemis Victor's conservative step-and-drag footwork is doing her no favours. Rachel Doricko wins the third round because, by using weird footwork, she was willing to take a chance. Like so many things in Rachel Doricko's life, this chance taking will turn out in her favour. But there will also be times when the chance taking leads her to failure. And Rachel Doricko will never truly be able to muster the gumption for dramatic chance taking on things outside of boxing. Rachel will become a grocery store manager. For a grocery store manager, a weird-hat philosophy is beneficial to deploy. A weird hat says, Don't talk to me while I'm shelving these Ritz crackers. A weird hat can also say, Don't waste my time. But, wonderfully, a weird hat can be something else besides a thing that is frightening and scary. A weird-hat philosophy, is, after all, just a filtering mechanism. There are those people who are not upset by weird hats when people wear them. Grocery store employees are, in general, not upset by weird hats. Grocery store employees have seen it all. For grocery store employees, a weird hat can even be reassuring. At least the person at hand's most freakish self has manifested itself into something as harmless as a piece of clothing. At least it's just a hat and not a weapon. By the time Rachel Doricko becomes a grocery store manager she even views her weird hats as a kind of protection. People are definitely less likely to hold up somebody who is wearing a hat that makes them look a little crazy. Rachel Doricko wishes she could tell what exactly makes Artemis Victor a little crazy. By virtue of her presence, and her unparalleled training and form and skill, Artemis Victor has to have something about her that is a little insane. Artemis Victor is good at boxing not because of her Victor sister inheritance, but because she is wildly jealous. Artemis Victor just wants to beat her eldest sister, Star Victor, who was previously a Daughters of America winner, and the only way for Artemis Victor to do that is to win this match, and then one after. Artemis Victor has to beat Rachel Doricko in order to advance. Rachel Doricko keeps punching Artemis Victor with her hands. The fourth round is called for Rachel, which evens the score to 2–2. As the fifth round begins, Artemis Victor remembers that she is a bucket of water. Artemis Victor thinks of the bodies that get pulled from rivers. Murdered and bloated, soaked so heavy that their hands look like medical gloves that have been blown into balloons, the people Artemis Victor beats are made into waterlogged relics. Artemis Victor didn't put lead in her gloves, but nobody checked her gloves this match. Maybe the judges wanted her to put lead in her gloves, thinks Artemis Victor. The judges all know her parents and her sisters. Maybe the judges were testing her, seeing if she is capable of murder. But Artemis Victor isn't interested in that type of murder. Artemis Victor is only interested in the slow murder of water. Artemis Victor wants to make Rachel Doricko drown.

•

As the fifth round begins, the other girl fighters enter the gym. Iggy Lang and Rose Mueller stand watching from separate corners. To Iggy Lang, it looks like this fight is a fight about aesthetics. Both Artemis Victor and Rachel Doricko are skilled and practised, but Artemis Victor has the punch of a perfectionist, whereas Rachel Doricko has the punch of a stylist. Rachel Doricko's footwork isn't a copy of someone else's but a strategy of her own invention. When Rachel Doricko moves her feet, she puts one foot in front of the other like the slow, steady advance of a wildfire. Her knees are bent and forward. Normally a fighter would keep their knees over their ankles, but Rachel Doricko has her knees leaning out more, slanted over her toes. It makes Rachel Doricko's whole body look like it's being held up against the wind. If I have to fight her, thinks Iggy Lang, I just need to find a way to make Rachel Doricko lean backwards instead of forwards. Rachel Doricko advances on Artemis Victor and leans even more heavily into a fictional wind. Artemis Victor moves to the left to avoid the slant. Still, Rachel Doricko is able to punch Artemis Victor with her hands.

•

Although Kate Heffer and Andi Taylor are not present, their successes and failures haunt this match. Parts of their souls are carried inside each boxer who beat them, as if Kate Heffer's and Andi Taylor's bodies, post-defeat, have been cannibalised by the victors as part of a ritual of war. Andi Taylor's dead red-truck kid lives inside Artemis Victor, and Rachel Doricko clenches Kate Heffer's counting numbers in her hands. Andi Taylor is speeding home to Tampa, her windows down, her gas cash hot in the back pocket of her jeans, but Andi Taylor is also pulsing inside Artemis Victor mid-swing. When Artemis Victor punches Rachel Doricko, it's like Artemis and Andi are doing the punching together. Artemis remembers the hole Andi punched through, and she has, for Rachel Doricko, had that hole cemented over. In her car, Andi Taylor is looking in her rearview mirror, and she keeps thinking she sees water. Andi Taylor is speeding through the long desert roads of Arizona, New Mexico, and Texas. She drives in silence. Andi Taylor wishes she had beaten Artemis Victor, but a part of her knows that there was not a world in which she could have triumphed over her. At least the body Andi Taylor touched is now touching Rachel Doricko in this second round. Just as Andi Taylor thinks this, back in Reno, Artemis Victor hits Rachel Doricko in the mouth.

•

The hit makes Rachel Doricko's teeth feel cool and electric. As Rachel Doricko advances back towards Artemis Victor her jaw clenches.

•

Andi Taylor will find a person who makes her relieved to be alive after she becomes a pharmacist. Even though Andi Taylor's life will be quiet, it will not lack for luminescence. Andi Taylor will have a dog named Freeway that can sit on its hind legs like a human on their knees stands. Andi Taylor and the person who makes her relieved to be alive will be lovers. They will not marry, and they will die separately, but they will spend the majority of their lives imagining what the other will look like when they're old. Before they separate, Andi Taylor and her lover will build a house with their own hands. It will be a stunning clay brick structure. On a hot summer day, when Andi Taylor is forty-two and lifting a large clay brick, Andi Taylor's lover will look at Andi's muscular, tank-top-clad shoulders, and think that it is not a wonder that Andi Taylor was once a boxer. Andi Taylor's boxing past seems, to Andi Taylor's lover, if not secret, then plastered over. It is wonderful that it is impossible to share your whole self with a lover, thinks Andi Taylor's partner. As Andi Taylor puts the brick in place, Andi Taylor's lover looks at Andi Taylor's knuckles and the veiny backs of her hands. These hands are the hands that once hit Artemis Victor. Andi Taylor never got to fight Kate Heffer, but because Andi Taylor's hands touched Artemis Victor, and because Artemis Victor's hands touched Rachel Doricko, who beat Kate Heffer, there is a connection between the hands of Andi Taylor and the hands of Kate Heffer. If the Daughters of America tournament bracket was flipped counterclockwise on its side, it would look like a family tree, and Andi Taylor, by way of marriage or blood, would be Kate Heffer's sister.

•

It is a wonder, thinks Kate Heffer as she is driving home to Seattle with her parents, that she had ever once been a victor. She might have lost to Rachel Doricko, but in the Pacific Northwest regionals she had been the winner. Perhaps, thinks Kate Heffer, I will have a future, and maybe in the future I can again be a victor? Weddings, thinks Kate Heffer, have so many rules and events. Their length, with a rehearsal dinner and morning-after brunch, is not so different from the length of a tournament. When Artemis Victor gets married, she'll wish she'd hired a Kate Heffer to make a solid, drama-free, but predictably glamorous plan. Kate Heffer's life will not have the opaline small glow of Andi Taylor's. Kate Heffer's life will be a life that looks like an hourglass filled with sand.

•

Having a life made out of sand will delight Kate Heffer. A grain of sand is a finite unit that can be quantified into countable numbers.

•

Artemis Victor had watched Kate Heffer after Kate Heffer lost her first-round match. Kate had looked so wet and tattered.

•

Artemis Victor has always and will always pride herself on being the highest and driest piece of land.

•

The slow drip of water is an incredibly violent weapon, but in order for a drip-of-water weapon to work it needs time. If one spills water on a wood floor it takes at least a day for the wood to start buckling. Compared to other sports, boxing matches are so short that there is not enough time for something slow-moving to activate. Eight two-minute rounds, with time-outs and pauses between rounds, is barely enough time for anything at all to happen. And yet, it seems like within each two-minute round, anything could happen. Rachel Doricko believes that time will move as fast or slow as it wants regardless of whether she walks through a specific instant. Artemis Victor, on the other hand, believes, like Kate Heffer, that events and time circle her, that time exists so she can walk through it. This inability to see that time is moving forward, and that there is not enough time to enact damage by water, will lose Artemis Victor this round, and the round after. By the sixth round the score is 4–2 in Rachel Doricko's favour. Rachel Doricko only needs to win one more round in order to become the winner.

•

As Rachel Doricko bounces in the corner, Kate Heffer, Rachel's cannibalised war trophy, bounces with her. The digits of pi bob up and down. They sound like a coin purse being jangled around.

•

Artemis Victor will be a victor in so many arenas of her life. She'll carry her ruthless drip with her forever. When the house she was house-sitting for melted from the broken pipe she was not filled with dread. This is not my house, Artemis Victor had thought, and Artemis Victor had known that the damage was not her fault, but the fault of the house's neglectful owners. Still, there are people, people like Rachel Doricko, who would enter the water-melted house and be filled with dread. The dread comes from the possibility that one might actually be responsible for the disaster. There are people who, just by looking at disasters, implicate themselves in the violence at hand. These people, the self-implicating people, are far less likely to be victors, but they are more emotionally intelligent, and more likely to be able to see details that others might miss. Rachel Doricko, unlike Artemis Victor, is a stylist. Rachel Doricko is not perfect. Like a ripped pair of jeans, Rachel Doricko has purposefully carved defects in her punches. There is not enough time in this match for the violence of water to take hold. Because of this, Rachel Doricko is able to hit Artemis Victor in the head. Rachel Doricko lands six hits in a row and then the round is over. Even though in the general arena of life Artemis Victor will so clearly be the winner, here in Reno, in this second-round, semi-finalist match, Rachel Doricko has taken over. When the bell rings to officially end the bout, Artemis Victor is a red-eyed puddle of water.

•

As Rachel Doricko stands tall and the referee pulls one of her gloved hands above her head, Rachel Doricko can hear her grandmother clapping for her. Rachel Doricko's coach and Artemis Victor's coach have already peeled away and are talking with one another. Artemis Victor does not approach Rachel Doricko and Rachel Doricko does not approach Artemis Victor. If that's how Artemis Victor wants to lose, thinks Rachel Doricko, be my guest. Rachel Doricko feels a warmth radiating through her chest. It's a warmth that she'll feel again very few times in her life. It's almost like love, but it has a surer, less desperate edge to it. It's the feeling she'll feel when, many decades in the future, her wife will ask her, smiling, why, with her weird hats, she always has to be so dramatic? Here in Reno, Rachel Doricko can be as dramatic as she likes. The sport of boxing calls for it. As she pulls the tape off her gloves with her teeth, she feels the hot burn of the next-bout girls' eyes watching her. Whoever wins the next match will have to be ready to face her.

•

Artemis Victor is dragged from the ring by her attentive parents. Puffy-eyed and devastated, Artemis Victor cannot believe that she was unable to beat Rachel Doricko with her hands. Artemis Victor had spent so much time looking in the mirror, boxing in front of her reflection. In the gym Artemis Victor and her sisters grew up in, there was one wall that was all mirrors, so that when you practised in the ring, or punched one of the body bags, you could, out of the corner of your eye, see your reflection. Artemis Victor knows how this loss looks on her and she cannot bear it. Artemis Victor's parents tell her to calm down and to watch the next match, but she cannot do it. Instead, Artemis Victor walks out the front door of Bob's Boxing Palace and sits in the family car. Artemis Victor sits in the passenger seat and pulls down the visor. On the visor is a little mirror. In the mirror Artemis Victor sees her smudged eye makeup and her swollen cheek and, behind her cheek, the skyline of downtown Reno off in the distance. Like the casinos on the Reno strip, the Daughters of America tournament will not make good on many of its promises.

IGGY LANG
VS.
ROSE MUELLER

Fountain Place is Rose Mueller's favourite building in Dallas. The skyscraper is flanked by 172 exterior fountains. Circular patches of earth with trees planted on the patches are scattered throughout the fountains like an archipelago of single-tree islands. At night, the fountains light up in a choreographed dance. When Rose Mueller was six, her father took her to see the fountains after the sun had set. The underwater lights made her feel like she might be able to breathe in something other than air. Rose Mueller remembers holding her father's hand in one hand and running her other hand through the water. Underneath the water there had been leaves and pennies and, somehow, sand. Where had the sand blown in from? And how had the water been able to stay so clear, and so blue, even at night?

•

When Rose Mueller stuck her arm in the fountain, she felt like she was straddling worlds, plunging her hand into a space portal while her body stayed crouched and small in downtown Dallas. The mirrored prism walls of the Fountain Place skyscraper had loomed above her head. She learned later that, when it was originally built, the architects of Fountain Place had intended to build it a twin, but then the price of oil had crashed so the second lot, the lot meant for the twin, stayed vacant. Her whole childhood Rose Mueller wondered if the unbuilt twin building would have been a true twin, or just an architectural sibling: another skyscraper with the same ideas in it but reshuffled and rotated to make it fresh. Shortly before Rose Mueller drove to Reno with her father, she heard her father say, after mass, that there were contracts going out for a Fountain Place twin building. The money had, suddenly, these many decades later, been found. As she and her father drove to Reno and Rose Mueller worked through the possible outcomes of the Daughters of America tournament in her head, the as-yet-unrealised twin Fountain Place building kept visiting Rose Mueller's mind. Here in the ring in Bob's Boxing Palace, puffed up and facing Iggy Lang like one would face their nemesis, Rose Mueller feels as though she might be looking at a relative. Iggy Lang has a purple lip, but both Rose Mueller and Iggy Lang have the muscles of well-trained dogs. Their limbs are svelte and athletic. Their arms look like, if you sliced them open, you would see a perfect medical diagram of all of their tendons. The first round begins, and Iggy Lang's right fist meets Rose Mueller's left shoulder. Iggy Lang is taller, but she is boxing squatting lower.

•

Rose Mueller hits right and then left, but Iggy Lang pulls back and the hits don't land. The onlookers in the gym can hear the air moving out of the way of Rose Mueller. When Rose Mueller punches the air there is a sound like the sound of swishing water.

•

The fourteen onlookers left in the gym include the *WYBA* journalist, the journalist from the local paper, Rose Mueller's father, Izzy Lang, and Izzy Lang's mother. Tanya Maw and Rachel Doricko are also here, but they're both watching the bout separately, spread out in the back.

Although Tanya Maw and Izzy Lang are not fighting today, their bodies, as losers to the current-bout fighters, haunt this match. Tanya Maw can see that Rose Mueller's form improved after fighting her. Rose Mueller used to lean to the left slightly when recovering from a hit, but now she is centred.

•

Tanya Maw and Izzy Lang are both watching this match in spite of being yesterday's losers. Rose Mueller boxes like a cement truck filling a building's foundation, thinks Izzy Lang. Izzy Lang wouldn't have stayed, except that she had to stay because she and Iggy are cousins. Tanya Maw drove herself from Albuquerque, so she could have left at any time. Tanya Maw stayed because she wants to know how the tournament is going to finish. She is genuinely curious. Tanya Maw would never leave a play before a play is finished.

•

In this first round, Iggy Lang's and Rose Mueller's bodies blur into one another. To the onlookers they look incredibly similar. Iggy Lang wishes she was still boxing against her older cousin, Izzy Lang, but here Iggy Lang is, boxing against Rose Mueller.

•

Iggy Lang will become a private investigator. When she first tells her parents about her choice of profession, they'll think it's a joke, but she'll explain that the money is good, that the hours are flexible, and that most of her clients are just disgruntled wives. It's fun, Iggy Lang will tell her parents. It's like school in that there are very definitive and finite projects.

•

One of the things that make Iggy Lang an excellent private investigator is that she has a face that no one could ever forget. Her purple lip makes her look like a survivor of an accident. Because people feel disarmed by her strange face, they're more willing to tell her their secrets. This built-in intimacy, combined with her expert online-stalking tactics, makes her one of Chicago's best. Izzy Lang, Iggy Lang's girl-boxer cousin of yore, and Iggy will live fairly close to each other, but the two once-fabled, girl-boxer cousins will mostly see each other only in Douglas, Michigan, when home visiting each of their families for the Fourth of July.

•

Rose Mueller extends her hand again and this time the hit lands. Iggy Lang looks surprised that the hit reached her, even though Rachel Doricko, and the other boxers left in the gym, were able to recognise immediately after Rose Mueller's hand had left the gate of her chest that it would land. Rose Mueller had somehow managed to move closer to Iggy Lang. It looked like Rose Mueller was breathing on her, or maybe even like Rose Mueller was whispering something to her. Both Rose Mueller's and Iggy Lang's mouth guards make their cheeks look like they have food stuffed in them. There is a game that both Rose Mueller and Iggy Lang grew up playing where they did have food stuffed in their cheeks. In the game, you stuff the insides of your cheeks with as many s'mores-sized marshmallows as you can. The person who is able to get the most marshmallows in their mouth, and still say the tongue twister 'chubby bunny', wins.

•

Like all games, there is an inherently wasteful aspect to Chubby Bunny. After the game is finished, the players spit everything out. A pile of saliva-soaked, bile-lined marshmallows makes a gooey white mound.

•

Rose Mueller lands another hit on Iggy Lang. It's a long reach of a hit that, when it finally gets to Iggy, makes a soft sound.

•

The spitting out of the marshmallows is one of the most fun parts of the game. The spitting is accompanied by incessant giggling. When the marshmallows leave the girls' mouths it looks like the girls are vomiting up soft, Renaissance fresco clouds. Iggy Lang and Izzy Lang will play Chubby Bunny every Fourth of July for the rest of their once young, and then adult lives.

•

Rose Mueller will play Chubby Bunny with her young son in Dallas. You have to put the first ones behind your back molars, she'll whisper to him. The only way to win Chubby Bunny is to use your saliva to partially dissolve them.

•

Fighting is the opposite of being in hiding, which, for Rose Mueller, is a challenge. Why didn't she pick an activity where she couldn't be seen, like playing in an orchestra pit or doing costumes for a school play? There is something about the necessity of being seen while boxing that frightens Rose Mueller. At any time, Iggy Lang could pick her up and go lock her in the coach's office over in the corner.

•

As Rose Mueller thinks this she shudders. In the space of time that she shakes, Iggy Lang hits her. It is genuinely unclear to all, even the most expert coaches, who will be the winner.

•

The journalist covering the tournament for the local Reno paper is rapt. Rose Mueller took the hit with such a stoic face. Like watching a mountain in an earthquake, it is clear the hit shook Rose, but it is also clear that the mountain is going nowhere. As Rose Mueller's coach watches this bout, he remembers the first day he taught her to box and he is doubtful of what he taught her. Rose Mueller does not box like an amateur.

•

Izzy Lang wants her cousin, Iggy Lang, to punch Rose Mueller in the face. These first few moments into the bout Izzy Lang has changed her mind. Izzy Lang does care who is the victor. She is glad that, because they share a ride, she has an excuse to stay and watch her younger kid-cousin boxer.

•

One of the most beautiful things Rose Mueller has ever seen is a nun playing improvisational jazz piano behind a curtain. It was a performance that her father took her to at the Meyerson Symphony Center in Dallas. The nun was world-famous. The nun played behind a curtain for the same reason that churches sometimes drape cloths over a saint's face. Rose Mueller wishes that there were sheets hanging from the ceiling of Bob's Boxing Palace that enclosed this match. Rose Mueller wishes she was fighting Iggy Lang inside a white cube of fabric. Rose Mueller might be able to hit Iggy Lang, if no one can see that Rose Mueller is hitting her. Rose Mueller tries to imagine that there is no one watching her. This works, and Rose Mueller lands seven hits quickly to win the first round. Iggy Lang and Rose Mueller separate briefly, and then walk back towards each other to begin the second round.

•

Rose Mueller's father did not suggest that Rose Mueller become a boxer. He had asked Rose, when she moved schools, if there was a sport she wanted to play. She was so big for her age. Maybe a sport will protect her, thought Rose Mueller's father. He hadn't expected that she would see a poster downtown advertising a class for young boxers.

•

When Rose Mueller's father asked her why she wanted to try boxing, Rose Mueller said she wanted to box because it seemed like a sport where the rules were clear at all times. In boxing, Rose Mueller told her father, it seems hard for there to be any mystery. In church, Rose Mueller thought to herself, there is so much mystery. I need to learn to be in a space where I can see people and understand what is going on in their minds.

•

When Iggy Lang looks at Rose Mueller, she can't read her. Usually, Iggy Lang thinks to herself, I can read my opponent by the way they stand. But Rose Mueller is changing her stance like a girl who, before she goes out, serially tries on different outfits. In the second round Rose Mueller lands four, then five, then nine punches. The second round also goes to Rose Mueller. Iggy Lang is pulling her purple lip up over her mouth guard, running her tongue in between her mouth guard and the interior of her upper lip. Izzy Lang can tell that Iggy Lang is furious.

•

Iggy Lang's coach says something to Iggy in between rounds, but Iggy bats her coach's language away, like she is swatting flies off a cut of meat.

•

As the third round begins, light slants in from the skylight. Wind shakes the thin tin walls of the gym, which interrupts the soft steady sounds of Iggy Lang punching Rose Mueller with her fists.

•

The water of Rose Mueller's childhood fish tank was much closer to green than the blue of the fountains in downtown Dallas. Rose Mueller had wanted a fish tank for the same reason that she liked the fountains, and the same reason she didn't really mind going to mass. Rose Mueller wanted to see if maybe there was another way to live in this world, and Rose Mueller wanted to see if there were other worlds to live in besides the suburbs of Dallas. The fish tank had been so green and mysterious. She had bought a dwarf sucking catfish to eat the algae from the glass. Here in Bob's Boxing Palace, Rose Mueller feels close to being underwater. She's not sure that either she or Iggy Lang is able to breathe underwater, but it seems equally implausible that the only thing they are breathing in this gym is air. Even in adulthood, the fountains of Fountain Place will provoke in Rose Mueller a feeling of departure. As she faces Iggy Lang, Rose Mueller thinks of the way that the fountains of Fountain Place seem to jump up from nowhere, the power that is pushing the water up and out hidden deep in the ground. Rose Mueller thinks of her arms not as a slow, controlled drip of water, but as a release valve of liquid ready to shoot up into the sky. Just as she thinks this, Iggy Lang lands a hit on her eye.

•

In boxing, a direct hit on an eye can be enough to end a match. But, by some magic, Rose Mueller's eye is unfazed. Rose Mueller's eye does begin to bruise, but her vision remains immaculate. She immediately returns Iggy Lang's punches.

•

Rose Mueller's eyes turn into hardened glass and her arms turn into fountains. She lands a run of eight direct hits, which finishes the round. This bout is like watching two people talking where one person is doing all of the mouth work, and only every once in a while, the other person interjects. Iggy Lang had to shout in order to get her black-eye punch through, but now Iggy Lang is being drowned out by Rose Mueller's fire hose of water. The score is 3–0 in Rose Mueller's favour. It's still possible for Iggy Lang to win, but more possible that Iggy Lang will be bounced out by Rose Mueller. Iggy Lang is young, and Iggy Lang is devastated that it's her in the ring instead of her cousin. Iggy Lang's not even sure she still wants to be the winner. Iggy Lang wishes she still wanted to win this tournament as bad as her dog wants to play fetch. Iggy Lang loves to box, but without the familial battle for love and respect, to Iggy Lang the sport feels empty and vapid. Iggy Lang realises that perhaps the only person she wanted to box against was her cousin.

•

Rose Mueller's crew-cut hair is so wet it looks like it's been cast in plastic.

•

The next time Rose Mueller looks at Iggy Lang, she realises that Iggy Lang is not a relative. Iggy Lang is present, but she also looks vacant. Iggy Lang has clearly left the match in some way, but Rose Mueller can't decipher to where Iggy Lang has left. Maybe Iggy Lang has a fountain or a fish tank or another world like the other worlds they talk about in mass, thinks Rose Mueller. Maybe Iggy Lang has left just so she can return, thinks Rose Mueller. Maybe Iggy Lang is sinking into water, thinks Rose Mueller. Maybe Iggy Lang's purple lip is proof that she is a fish.

•

Fish can grow purple spots on their lips. The spots are usually proof that the fish are sick or dying. One of the only ways to cure a spotted lip on a fish is to pour antibacterial medicine in their tank. If Iggy Lang is a fish, she is having a hard time breathing underwater. There is something in the air at Bob's Boxing Palace that is not agreeing with her.

•

In between the third and fourth rounds Rose Mueller's eye does not swell, but a circle of black blood pools under her skin. The immediacy of her black eye makes Rose Mueller look like a war veteran. Iggy Lang is envious of the face that she has given to her. Rose Mueller's black eye looks like a ring of slim waxy petals from a purple wildflower.

•

When Iggy Lang watched Rose Mueller and Tanya Maw box each other Iggy Lang had not fully processed the viciousness with which Rose Mueller used her fists. Perhaps it had been because Iggy Lang was so focused on recording Rose Mueller's stance, or perhaps it was because Rose Mueller actually looked kind. When Rose Mueller beat Tanya Maw there had been no anger in her eyes.

•

At night, when one walks through the fountains of Fountain Place in downtown Dallas, it is almost always deserted, save one or two people who are unhoused. The reality of a skyscraper being built in a boomtown that is as flat and suburban and spread out as Dallas is that the skyscraper keeps business hours like the hours of a bank. Hours outside banking hours end up being empty and closed down. These outside hours are Rose Mueller's favourite hours to visit. Throughout her life in Dallas, her village of life and then death, Rose Mueller will visit the fountains when the rest of downtown is closed down. She can feel herself so close to being able to breathe underwater. Unlike the other girls of the Daughters of America tournament, Rose Mueller might be amphibious. She is able to exist in mass and outside of it. The gym Rose Mueller will eventually own with her husband is proof of her ability to shape-shift her own physical environment. Rose Mueller is good at taking one environment and making it into another. Perhaps, thinks Rose Mueller, if I can flood Bob's Boxing Palace, I can be the winner.

•

The fourth round begins, and Iggy Lang is jittery. Her legs look like they have been shocked with electricity. A blue vein is popping out of her right arm. The vein looks like a baby snake is living in her arm.

•

Rose Mueller's black eye gets even blacker. Her black eye seems to emanate a new power. Like war paint, Rose Mueller's black eye shows the parents and the other girl boxers and the journalists and the coaches and the judges that she had been hit with the worst punch and survived. Good luck to anyone, including Iggy Lang, who ever hoped to make Rose Mueller cry.

•

Iggy Lang can't even remember why she wanted to win this tournament. Without Izzy Lang, her older cousin, it all seems so sappy and stupid and dramatic. Izzy hadn't even wanted to come to watch Iggy's semi-finalist match. What use is having a cousin who also boxes if your cousin isn't interested in being a family of legend? Izzy Lang could keep boxing after the Daughters of America tournament in a new, older age bracket, but when Izzy doesn't, Iggy won't be entirely sad. In order for Iggy to be a victor she will have to learn how to build her world of boxing without her cousin. Iggy Lang will have to learn to box with total abandon. All Iggy Lang has at her disposal right now is her purple lip. Rose Mueller punches her three times and Iggy Lang is unable to return a hit.

•

Rose Mueller is surprised by Iggy Lang's lack of endurance. Rose Mueller would have thought that always having a cousin to train with would have helped Iggy Lang's ability to rally through a match. Instead, Iggy Lang is all but finished. When Rose Mueller fakes left and then hits right, she lands three more punches.

•

The next two rounds Rose Mueller beats Iggy Lang with the certainty of someone saying the call-and-response lyrics of mass. One cannot lose harder than 5–0 in a match. Iggy Lang looks up to the ceiling and closes her eyes. She ducks out of the ring, spits her mouth guard out, and sits on the ground. Iggy Lang wishes she was a dog, or a statue of a dog, or a statue of a war hero. Dogs and statues don't have to use language to talk with people. Rose Mueller walks over to shake Iggy Lang's hand, but Iggy Lang refuses to take it. There are no rules about what one has to do after a match in the Women's Youth Boxing Association.

•

Rose Mueller exits the ring like she is crossing the border from sandy beach to water.

•

In this break between bouts, Rose Mueller does not pray. When Rose Mueller drops to her knees and brings her palms together in front of her chest she is faking. When Rose Mueller pretends to pray, what she is really doing is observing.

•

Praying in public is like draping oneself in a sheet. It is an activity that makes one absent. Inside absent activities it is possible to look more closely at one's environment.

•

While Rose Mueller pretends to pray, she watches Rachel Doricko fiddle with her hat. The hat is made of fur and looks hot and ragged. Rachel Doricko's back looks strong, but the way that Rachel Doricko holds her rib cage over her hips is slanted.

•

The final round will take place later in the afternoon, after the judges break for lunch.

•

When Rose Mueller returns from lunch her eye is a black spill of oil. Her eye is shiny and slick. Nobody in Rose Mueller's church could have imagined this. Would the people of God, or the people who claim to be the people of God, condone Rose Mueller hitting someone with her fists?

•

Rose Mueller did beat Iggy Lang, but Rose Mueller isn't thinking in exactly the right order. In the moments before the last bout of the tournament Rose Mueller's memory is not linear.

•

Rose Mueller imagines crossing over into the next match like a salamander walking from land into the water. Even with her headgear off, Rose Mueller feels like her head has been dunked in a bucket. It's blistering hot in the gym. It's blistering hot everywhere in Reno. Rose Mueller can see the heat waves wafting off the ground through a window.

•

The twin Fountain Place skyscraper building in Dallas will be built, but it will not have fountains.

•

As Rose Mueller waits for the championship match to begin she watches the way the dust in the gym sparkles like sequins. Like the suburbs of Dallas, Bob's Boxing Palace is not glamorous, but there is a festive red banner in the gym that reads THE 12TH ANNUAL DAUGHTERS OF AMERICA CUP. The banner is printed on shiny laminate. There is a trophy for the winner that sits on the folding card table where the judges eat. The trophy is a small plastic-gold cup. The cup is affixed to a four-by-four plaqueless marble stand. Light bounces off the cup and falls to the ground. As Rose Mueller walks by the folding card table on her way to re-enter the ring for the championship match, she sees that there is no way that the Daughters of America Cup trophy would ever hold water. There is a slit in the cup where the plastic mould came together.

JULY 15

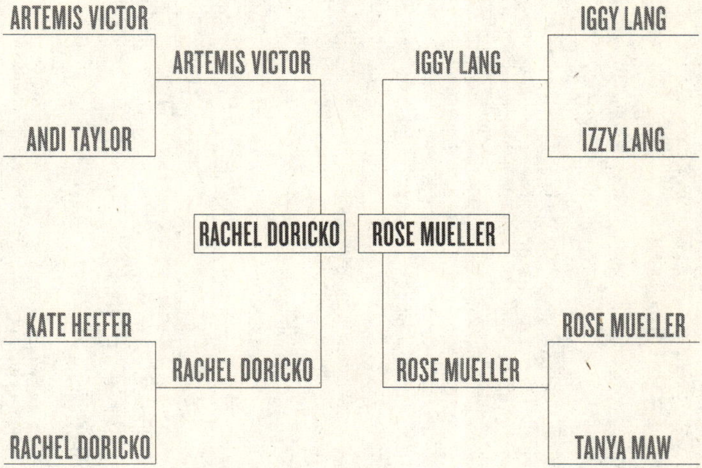
ARTEMIS VICTOR
ANDI TAYLOR
ARTEMIS VICTOR
KATE HEFFER
RACHEL DORICKO
RACHEL DORICKO
RACHEL DORICKO
ROSE MUELLER
IGGY LANG
IGGY LANG
IZZY LANG
ROSE MUELLER
ROSE MUELLER
TANYA MAW

RACHEL DORICKO
VS.
ROSE MUELLER

The name of the local Reno journalist covering the Daughters of America tournament is Sam. Sam works for the *Reno Gazette-Journal*. He usually manages the obituaries and writes about high school basketball. Sam has watched every match of this tournament with the awe of a sceptic witnessing a miracle. The girls of the Daughters of America tournament fight like they are assassins. When they walk through the gym in between rounds, the dusty air parts in front of each of them like water parting for a god. The girls all look different, and the way each of them boxes is distinct, but there is something collective about their energy. Sitting in a white folding chair, waiting for the championship match to begin, Sam thinks about how something about the Daughters of America tournament feels like a game played in reverse. Usually, as a tournament progresses, there is a feeling of whittling, of a group of many reduced to a single champion, but here in Bob's Boxing Palace, at the Daughters of America tournament, as each bout has been fought, there has been the feeling of accumulation. Even though only Rachel Doricko and Rose Mueller are in the ring, Sam keeps thinking he sees the shadows of the other girl boxers. The overhead floodlights in Bob's Boxing Palace cast multiple shadows from the same body. Rachel Doricko and Rose Mueller look so tall and sturdy. They look powerful, but they also look bruised and beat and weathered from their preceding fights yesterday and today. As the first round begins, and Rachel Doricko hits Rose Mueller on the shoulder, Sam remembers a game that he used to play with his cousins and his sister. At different points in these first moments of the bout, Rose Mueller and Rachel Doricko defend themselves by walking backwards. To begin a game of Sardines, Sam remembers, one person hides, while a group of people close their eyes, and then the individuals of the group go in search of the person in hiding. It's like hide-and-go-seek, but in reverse. One by one the seekers find, and then join, the hider. In the end of Sardines there is always one final person, alone, wandering around, looking for the group that began the game. The final person to find the group is technically the loser, but when the final person finds the group, all the players make a loud celebratory sound. Rachel Doricko and Rose Mueller are both mercilessly searching for a hole through which they can hit each other's faces. Rose Mueller unleashes a leaping left hook onto Rachel Doricko's side. Sam sees a spray of sweat pop off when the hit lands. The sweat droplets sparkle like a shower of diamonds. When Artemis Victor had boxed, there had been a slow drip about her. Something small and measured. Sam had read in the *WYBA* magazine, when preparing to cover the Daughters of America tournament, that Artemis Victor was from Redding, California, a place Sam remembered as being near Shasta, where the land is littered with limestone-drip caves. Inside the caverns near Artemis Victor's hometown, limestone drips make sixty-foot icicle spikes that hang from the ceiling and grow up out of the ground. Sam visited them while on a nature vacation. He had taken a tour while visiting Redding. The drip formations reaching for each other looked like rocks in the process of kissing. It made sense to Sam that Artemis Victor came from a place with caves that made you feel like you were living on another planet. When Artemis Victor and Andi Taylor boxed each other, Sam had felt like he was watching two aliens. Here in the championship match, Rachel Doricko's saliva is leaking out of her mouth. Rachel Doricko and Rose Mueller circle one another. They are both so quick at moving out of the way of each other's fists that there are, in this match, very few point-earning hits. There had been so many hits when Rachel Doricko had beaten that girl from Seattle, Kate Heffer. When Iggy Lang and Izzy Lang fought each other, the points had been more spread out, but then when Rose Mueller beat Tanya Maw, and when Rose Mueller beat Iggy Lang, it had been like watching a car get crushed by a falling boulder. Here, in the championship match, Rachel Doricko and Rose Mueller look like the opposite of someone smashed under a boulder. Rachel Doricko and Rose Mueller look like monuments. They both stand in the ring with their headgear and their mouth guards and their taped-on gloves and their lace-up shoes as if adorned in the ceremonial garb of a monarchy. Rachel Doricko has a strangeness about her form that might upset a less creative, less skilled boxer.

But Rose Mueller is an incredibly skilled boxer. Earlier today, Rose Mueller beat Iggy Lang with the definitiveness of a student turning in a sure-to-be-A-grade term paper. Sam snaps a picture. In the picture, Rachel Doricko and Rose Mueller are standing apart from one another, with their fists up in front of their faces, and their torsos leaning over their knees. The round is narrowly called for Rachel Doricko, but then the next round is called for Rose Mueller. The rounds go back and forth like this, as if Rose Mueller and Rachel Doricko are having an argument. The details of their debate are elegant. Rose Mueller and Rachel Doricko keep swapping round victories as if they are collaborative painters taking turns on the same canvas. Rachel Doricko boxes with the quick strokes of an impressionist, whereas Rose Mueller boxes with the detail of a photorealist. When the score reaches 4–4 the judges announce that there will have to be an overtime round. The round begins with Rose Mueller and Rachel Doricko moving out of the way of each other's fists with rapid precision. Rose Mueller and Rachel Doricko repeatedly make the spaces where their bodies once were vacant. Then, Rose Mueller lands a hit. Rose Mueller is midair when the hit lands. Both of Rose Mueller's feet had left the ground. Right before

Rose Mueller's toes touch the mat again, Rose Mueller lands another hit to finish the round. This second punch will be the last thing Rose Mueller feels before her feet return to the earth with a soft, gentle landing. Rose Mueller's lungs are contracting and expanding with great energy. It looks like she is inflating and deflating rapidly. In between breaths, Rose Mueller's gloved hand is raised above her head. Rose Mueller spits her mouth guard onto the ground. Without her mouth guard in, Rose Mueller smiles. Rose Mueller was once the best girl in the United States at boxing. In the article Sam published in the *Reno Gazette-Journal*, he wrote: Today, Rose Mueller need not dream of winning.

A NEWSPAPER CLIPPING

Rachel Doricko's grandmother will seek out, and order by mail, a copy of Sam's article in the *Reno Gazette-Journal*. Rachel Doricko's grandmother will clip out the article and gift it to Rachel, who will keep it in a folder under her bed. When Rachel's fifty-two, her daughter will find the clipping by chance. Rachel Doricko's daughter will ask Rachel, Who is the other girl in the picture? That's Rose Mueller, Rachel Doricko will say to her daughter. The day that that picture was taken Rose Mueller was, out of all girls in the country, the best boxer. Boxing against Rose Mueller felt like fighting someone who was telepathic. She knew where my fists were going to go before my punches even landed. Her body was so muscular it looked like it was made of hardened plastic. Hitting Rose Mueller's body with my fists felt like touching something that was electric. She had short hair, and her face was round and soft, and when she won the championship match, she looked at me. Those were the days I was wearing a hat that had a raccoon tail on it. If I met her now, who's to say if she would recognise me.

THE FUTURE

Girls are born with all of the eggs they will ever make. Tiny future fighters are nested inside the infant bodies of baby girls. Men are dead ends, but girls are infinite backwards and forwards. Like looking at one's reflection in two facing mirrors, it is impossible to say where the first female athlete began and where they will end. The Daughters of America tournament will not go on forever. The Women's Youth Boxing Association, like so many institutions before it, will crumble and then resurrect itself with a new face.

In 393 AD the Olympics were banned for being too pagan.

•

Rose Mueller imagined a uterus as heaven. A doctor once described a caesarean section to Rose Mueller as fishing for a body in a pool of blood. When Rose Mueller dies in her seventies, her son and husband at her side in a hospital in Dallas, she'll imagine her body lying in a red sticky puddle, sinking slowly into the viscous.

•

The deeper she sinks the redder the wet is, until she can feel the red on all sides and she sees only red when she blinks her eyes.

•

Like a boxing match, the backwards and forwards movements of how girl fighters spring up over time is not linear. Rose Mueller does not immediately get reborn as another girl fighter. Rather, each girl born has the ability to be activated into a boxer. When Artemis Victor and Andi Taylor and Iggy Lang and Izzy Lang and Rachel Doricko and Kate Heffer and Tanya Maw all age out of the Daughters of America tournament they will immediately be replaced by new fighters. For decades, girl fighters will fight inside Bob's Boxing Palace. Hundreds of girls will throw innumerable punches. The years will fold on themselves. Girls will continue to flock from all parts of the country to try their hand. Before every bout, the judges will look into the girls' gloves to check for lead. Eventually, the sport of boxing will wane because war and drought have made it difficult for recreational sports to happen. Bob's Boxing Palace, and the whole of Reno, will be abandoned. The tin walls of Bob's gym will collapse. New nations will be formed. People will live on other planets. On one of the new planets there will be a girl who reads the story of how Rome was founded, how the twin brothers, Romulus and Remus, survived infancy only because they were suckled by a she-wolf who found them floating down a river in a basket. On the new planet, the girl wonders if she might be an animal. The girl wonders why the she-wolf saved the boys, especially given that, after all of the she-wolf's efforts, Romulus ended up killing his brother out of greed. Maybe the she-wolf just wanted someone to play with, thinks the girl on the new planet. Maybe the she-wolf was just looking for someone with whom she could roll around. How are my hands like and unlike the paws of an animal? the girl on the new planet will wonder. Maybe there is another girl on this planet who is willing to play hand-clapping games with me? the girl on the new planet will wonder. The girl on the new planet will find a girl-mate so that she can play clapping games with her hands. The two girls will argue about the authenticity of the hand-clapping lyrics. One girl will hit another, and then the girls will be fighting each other with their hands. The two girls will circle each other like birds of prey. One girl squats low, puts her hands forward, and bares her teeth. The gums of her mouth are red. Her teeth are white and crooked. Down her back is one long thick braid. Six purple moons loom in the sky. When the girl lunges forward to reach the other girl, she misses, stumbles, readjusts her feet, and then the two girls lock eyes.

Thanks are owed to the following:

Institutions

The Whiting Foundation

MacDowell

Hawthornden Castle

Agents

Kristina Moore

Katie Cacouris

Jin Auh

Luke Ingram

Advocates

Oscar Villalon, Editor of ZYZZYVA, who published an excerpt of this book in 2019

Jill Meyers, Editor of A Strange Object, who first published *Belly Up*

Diane Williams, Editor of NOON, whose encouragement and generosity sustain me

Michael Silverblatt, host of Bookworm, who engaged with my work with unparalleled insight and grace

The Translators, Editors, and Publishers Who Have Brought My Writing Across Borders

Sara Reggiani of Edizioni Black Coffee, Italy

Leonardo Taiuti of Edizioni Black Coffee, Italy

Daniela Guglielmino of Bollati Boringhieri, Italy

Nektarios Lampropoulos of Haramada, Greece

Maria Christou of Haramada Publications, Greece (1973–2023)

Luc de Rooy, Belgium

Friederike Schilbach of Aufbau, Germany

Christiane Neudecker of Aufbau, Germany

My Editors at Viking

Paul Slovak

Allie Merola

Teachers

Laura van den Berg

Lorrie Moore

Nancy Reisman

Adrianne Harun

Friends Who Were Generous, Early Readers of this Book

Patrick Cottrell

Rebekah Bergman

Karina Mudd

Gillian Brassil

Joanna Howard

Maria Anderson

Mimi Lok

Friends Who Live Far from Me

Elana Siegal

Laura MacMillan

Shanoor Seervai

Meg Weeks

Friends Who Live Near to Me

Peggy Lee

Shanna Farrell

Lindsay Albert

Jenna Garrett, especially for the stunning images she gifted this book project

Sara Fan

Léonie Guyer

Mac McGinnes (1939–2022)

Nathaniel Dorsky

Family

Barbara Lombardi
Audrey Bullwinkel
Clay Bullwinkel
Denise Bullwinkel
Alex Spoto
Lucia Spoto
Elora Spoto
Angelo Spoto
Mary T. Spoto
Wes Hall
Naia Hall

My Brilliant Daunt Books Editor

Marigold Atkey

The Team at Daunt

Marsha Swan, Typesetter
Becca Calf, Assistant Editor
Jimena Gorráez, Publicist
Luke Bird, Cover Designer